"You realize," the Earl said, "that my cousin is almost insane about his desire to be rid of me?"

"Then what can we do?" Nola asked.

"That is what I am waiting for you to tell me," the Earl answered. "You saved me once and now I regard you as my keeper. And quite frankly, Nola, I am afraid to be without you."

"We will think of something. I am sure we will think of something," Nola said reassuringly.

At the same time she knew it was going to be very difficult . . .

A Camfield Novel of Love by Barbara Cartland

"Barbara Cartland's novels are all distinguished by their intelligence, good sense, and good nature. . . ."
— **ROMANTIC TIMES**

"Who could give better advice on how to keep your romance going strong than the world's most famous romance novelist, Barbara Cartland?"
— **THE STAR**

Camfield Place,
Hatfield
Hertfordshire,
England

Dearest Reader,

Camfield Novels of Love mark a very exciting era of my books with Jove. They have already published nearly two hundred of my titles since they became my first publisher in America, and now all my original paperback romances in the future will be published exclusively by them.

As you already know, Camfield Place in Hertfordshire is my home, which originally existed in 1275, but was rebuilt in 1867 by the grandfather of Beatrix Potter.

It was here in this lovely house, with the best view in the county, that she wrote *The Tale of Peter Rabbit*. Mr. McGregor's garden is exactly as she described it. The door in the wall that the fat little rabbit could not squeeze underneath and the goldfish pool where the white cat sat twitching its tail are still there.

I had Camfield Place blessed when I came here in 1950 and was so happy with my husband until he died, and now with my children and grandchildren, that I know the atmosphere is filled with love and we have all been very lucky.

It is easy here to write of love and I know you will enjoy the Camfield Novels of Love. Their plots are definitely exciting and the covers very romantic. They come to you, like all my books, with love.

Bless you,

CAMFIELD NOVELS OF LOVE
by Barbara Cartland

A NEW CAMFIELD NOVEL OF LOVE BY

Barbara Cartland

Three Days to Love

J

JOVE BOOKS, NEW YORK

THREE DAYS TO LOVE

A Jove Book / published by arrangement with
the author

PRINTING HISTORY
Jove edition / February 1996

The Putnam Berkley World Wide Web site address is
http://www.berkley.com

ISBN: 0-515-11812-5

A JOVE BOOK®
Jove Books are published by The Berkley Publishing Group,
200 Madison Avenue, New York, New York 10016.
JOVE and the "J" design are trademarks
belonging to Jove Publications, Inc.

PRINTED IN THE UNITED STATES OF AMERICA

10 9 8 7 6 5 4 3 2 1

Author's Note

GENERAL Gordon is one of the great heroes of British history and will never be forgotten while there are writers who find his life deeply moving.

He first made his name as a Commander of irregular troops in China.

He was a deeply religious, if unorthodox, Christian.

He was born in 1833 at Woolwich when his Father, General H. W. Gordon, of the Royal Artillery, was Inspector of the carriage department.

Charles George Gordon was the fourth son of a large family.

In the Crimean War he proved himself as an exceptionally intelligent and courageous Subaltern.

When he became Governor General of the Sudan, he agreed to do so after much hesitation and the toss of a coin.

He acquired sole responsibility for more than one million square miles filled with savage and hostile peoples, amongst which were to be found poverty, warfare, and the slave trade.

General Gordon wrote home, "I go up alone with an infinite Almighty God to direct and guide me."

Everyone knows the rest of the pathetic story.

He was instructed to evacuate the Sudan and establish an organised Government there.

He reached Khartoum on February 18th, 1884, and succeeded in evacuating 2,000 women and children besides the sick and wounded before the *Mahdi*'s forces closed in on the town.

Historians will always find it difficult to understand why at that time the British Government refused all urgent requests from the man it had despatched single-handed on the forlornest of forlorn hopes.

The prolonged procrastination made disaster inevitable.

It was not until August, after a long delay and intervention by the Queen, that a small force under Lord Wolsey set out from Wadi Haifa.

The resistance of Khartoum until January 26th, 1885, is one of the most remarkable achievements in military history.

It was due to the skill and indomitable spirit with which Gordon inspired and dominated the feeble Egyptian garrison.

After learning of two victories won by Lord Wolsey, the *Mahdi*'s troops were on the verge of raising the siege.

But again an unaccountable delay of the relief force encouraged them to make a final assault at a gap in the ramparts.

The garrision was butchered and General Gordon with them.

The relief force reached Khartoum three days too late.

Three Days to Love

chapter one

1886

"Yer've never heard such goings on, Miss Nola! Laughin', talkin', an' o'course drinkin' in th' Dinin'-Room 'til nigh on midnight an' th' ladies with dresses that low they might as well be naked! I don't know what yer poor Mother would have said if 'er were still alive, that I don't."

As Mrs. Kettle finished what she was saying, she flounced out of the room carrying a bucket of ashes from the fireplace.

Nola sighed.

She was well aware that she must not encourage Mrs. Kettle to talk like this about the new Earl.

At the same time, it was impossible to stop her. She could understand too that the whole village was agog.

They had waited a long time for the sixth Earl of Hallington to come to the country.

They had heard about his riotous parties in London.

There was always someone who knew one of the servants at another house.

They either wrote and told them what was happening or came to Hallington village to visit one of their relatives.

In fact, Nola had often thought, since the Earl had returned from abroad and claimed his title, that no-one had talked of anything else.

She knew it was wrong and unfair, but she could not helping feeling resentful.

He had been one of the Relief Force who had been unable to save General Gordon.

Ever since Nola had been a child, General Gordon had been her hero.

She could just remember her Father talking about what a success he had been as the Commander of irregular troops in China.

Then he had been Governor-General of the Sudan for the Khedive of Egypt.

After that came the tragedy and drama of his virtually single-handed defence of Khartoum.

Nola could not think about it without shedding tears.

General Gordon had been deeply religious.

This was perhaps why Nola's Father, the Reverend Mark Brackley, had been so interested in him.

Nola had grown up continually hearing his name, almost as if he were a close friend or relative.

Then, last year, he had been given the extraordinary, dangerous, and improperly expanded mission to evacuate the women and children from Khartoum.

Nola could remember when she first heard of an obscure *Fakir* who called himself the *Mahdi*.

He declared a Holy war, which her Father said was nonsense, and started to overrun provinces in the Sudan.

When General Gordon went out to oppose him,

it was thought there would be no more trouble from the *Mahdi*.

By what Nola's Father called a miracle, the General succeeded in evacuating 2,000 women and children and a great number of sick and wounded before the *Mahdi*'s forces closed in on the town.

It was then that a large number of English, like the Vicar of Hallington, found the British Government's behaviour unbelievable.

They refused all urgent requests from General Gordon for help!

It was only after public opinion and the newspapers began to protest every day in furious terms that the Government finally gave way.

The siege of Khartoum commenced in March.

It was not until August, under increasing pressure from the public, supported by angry expostulations from the Queen, that it was agreed that some steps, still underfined, should be made to relieve General Gordon.

In November a Relief Force under Lord Wolseley was sent out, but it was doomed to failure.

Nola and her Father and the whole village prayed ceaselessly that Khartoum would continue to resist the *Mahdi*'s troops.

But the unaccountable delay of the Relief Force encouraged the *Mahdi* to make a final assault at a gap in the ramparts.

When Nola heard the news that the garrison had been butchered and General Gordon killed, she burst into tears.

It seemed too cruel that the Relief Force had reached Khartoum exactly three days too late.

It was not only General Gordon for whom she, her Father, and the village had prayed, but also for a young man who had been with him—

William, the Viscount Ling, son and heir of the 5th Earl.

Nola had known William ever since she had been a child.

She was only three when he had put her in front of his saddle and taken her riding round the Park.

He was a charming young man, and everyone on the Estate and in the village loved him.

The only tragedy was he had no brothers or sisters.

William went to Eton and Oxford and brought his friends home in the holidays.

They were all extremely kind to the pretty little girl from the Vicarage.

Because the Earl was so fond of her Father, Nola was allowed to come and go as she pleased in the Big House.

When she was older she was allowed to ride any of the horses in the stables.

Hallington Hall was a large Estate and had a beautiful garden.

Nola often thought how lucky she was to enjoy the freedom of what was to her a fairy-land.

Those on the Estate all spoilt her.

The gardeners gave her the first peaches when they ripened.

At the Home Farm there were always brown eggs that were kept for "Miss Nola."

The Cook at the Big House made her birthday and Christmas cakes.

There was always something sweet and succulent waiting for her in the Kitchen.

When William was killed, Nola felt she had lost the only brother she had ever known, because she, too, was an only child.

"How could they have been so slow in relieving General Gordon, Papa?" she had asked over and over again.

'To be three days late,' she thought, 'was worse than if they had said it was impossible to get through at all.'

As her Father said:

"It was the English Government who killed General Gordon and William, not the *Mahdi*."

After William's death, the Earl felt he had nothing to live for, having lost his wife five years earlier and being in ill health for some time.

He was found dead one Sunday morning when his Valet went to call him to go to early Communion.

The Vicar buried him, and a small number of his relatives attended the funeral.

It was only then that Nora asked who was the heir.

It was some time before her Father received the answer.

As there was no direct Heir-Apparent, the Vicar learned that it was a distant Cousin who lived in the North of England.

As far as he could remember, the 5th Earl had never been in touch or spoken of this relative.

"Strangely enough," the Vicar said to his daughter, "there were two claimants for the title."

"Two?" Nola exclaimed.

"The Earl's Cousin Lionel," her Father explained, "died twenty years ago and never dreamt of succeeding to the title. He had twin sons!"

Nola was listening intently.

"Lionel and Michael," the Vicar continued, "both married and both had sons born within a few days of each other."

"How odd!" Nola murmured.

"The Solicitors have now agreed that Lionel's

5

son Rollo is the eldest, although Michael's son, David, tried to claim the title."

"Surely that was embarrassing?" Nola remarked.

"I suppose it was," her Father agreed, "but I personally am glad that Rollo is the 6th Earl, as he was in Lord Wolseley's Relief Force. They arrived too late to rescue General Gordon—but at least they tried."

From that moment Nola felt she disliked Rollo Ling, although she admitted to herself it was unfair.

She soon had, however, many other reasons for disliking him.

Her Father learnt from the Solicitors that he was wounded in the battle of Khartoum.

He was sent home, and it was only then he learned of William's death in Khartoum.

As he was treated for his injuries by surgeons in London, he found it extremely convenient to open Ling House in Park Lane.

It had been used only occasionally by William when he was up at Oxford and later before he left England to join General Gordon.

It was, Nola knew, a large house in which the late Earl, when he first married, had entertained extensively with his wife.

She was a great beauty and enjoyed being admired and fêted.

It was only after her death that the Earl had closed the house in London, taking no further interest in it.

Now, however, Nola, and, of course, the villagers, heard that the 6th Earl of Hallington was entertaining large parties night after night in the big Dining-Room.

There was dancing and gambling in the Reception Rooms in which the Countess had looked so beautiful.

When Nola said she thought it was an extraordinary way to behave, her Father replied:

"From what I hear, Rollo's Father was always very hard up. I can understand that, for a young man who has always had to count every penny, to suddenly find himself the 6th Earl of Hallington is a very exciting experience."

"Surely, Papa, now that he was recovered from his wounds, he will come down and see his Estate and at least take an interest in the family house?"

"I expect he will do so in due course," the Vicar said. "But if his new position has gone slightly to his head, we must be charitable enough to understand it."

'It was so like her Father,' Nola thought, 'to make excuses for the Earl.'

As Vicar he never refused to help anyone who came to him in trouble.

Because he was ostensibly a happy man, he made other people who came into contact with him happy too.

"I count my blessings," he said once to Nola, "and the biggest blessing I have at the moment is you, my precious daughter. I thank God every day because you are mine."

"That is a lovely thing to say, Papa," Nola answered, "but at the same time, you were much too kind to Farmer Johnston when you found he was cheating the people to whom he sold his crops."

The Vicar sighed.

"There are always," he said, "those in the world who are too greedy."

"And other people are too generous," Nola said pointedly.

Her Mother had often said that her Father

would take his shirt off his back and give it to a man who needed it more than he did.

When she was ill, she said to Nola:

"Look after your Father, Darling, you know he cannot look after himself."

"And that is why we need you, Mama," Nola had said.

Her Mother had smiled and patted her hand.

She knew the Doctors could do nothing for her, and she was dying slowly.

Nola was aware it was only her Father's religion and his belief in an afterlife that kept him from breaking down when his beloved wife was taken from him.

She had done everything she could to comfort him.

She knew, however, that a daughter could never mean the same as a wife, no matter how much her Father loved her.

Now he had to go North unexpectedly because he had learned that his brother was very ill.

Over sixty, it was so long since he had come South or they had been able to go North that Nola could hardly remember what he looked like.

She understood, however, that her Father felt he must be where he was most wanted.

She had promised to look after the village and everything else for as long as he was away.

The Services in the Church were taken by the Parson from the next village.

She had no intention of prying into what she thought were the private affairs of the small community in which they lived.

What she had not expected was that three days after her Father had left, word came from London.

The Earl intended to bring a party of friends to stay in Ling Hall on the following Friday.

The commotion this announcement caused was unbelievable.

After the 5th Earl had died, no-one had been given any orders.

Nor did any of the family appear to take the slightest interest in what was happening at the Hall.

There was a very old Manager of the Estate who had threatened for some years to retire.

He consulted the Vicar and they both thought the best thing before they heard from the new Earl was to let the younger servants find jobs elsewhere.

When the 5th Earl had died, his successor was still on his way back from Khartoum.

Later, when he reached England, he was in hospital.

The Manager and the Vicar, therefore, just carried on until he was well enough to take over.

However, when Rollo was well enough, he showed no interest in Ling Hall.

Reports just informed those in the country that he was "living it up," as the servants called it, and had no intention of leaving London.

"Do you think you ought to get in touch with him, Papa?" Nola asked.

"Certainly not," the Vicar replied. "It is not my business, and, if he has any instructions, he can make them through Mansfield, who, I assure you, is eagerly waiting for them."

Mr. Mansfield was the old Manager, and Nola knew that because he was so old, he wished to be left in peace.

What he had not expected, nor had anyone else, was that they were told on Tuesday that the Earl was arriving on Friday.

All the main rooms in the house had been shut up.

As Mrs. Chambers had asked hysterically:

"How can I get it all clean when there is no-one to do the cleaning?"

It was Nola who helped her when everyone else lost their heads.

She called on all the houses in the village that had a young girl.

They were astonished at her request that they should go up to the Big House immediately and help Mrs. Chambers.

Nola produced six housemaids who, even though they did not know their job, would do what they were told.

She also provided old Newman, the Butler who had been at the Hall for thirty years, with four footmen.

"You will have to tell them everything you want them to do," Nola said. "Dress them up in uniform and, as you know, there is a room in the attic full of them. At least they will look the part."

"I don't know whether I'm on me head or me heels, Miss Nola," Newman said, "and that's th' truth."

Even though they grumbled, they could not help feeling excited.

After all these years of nothing happening, the balloon had suddenly gone up.

"At least," one of them said, "we'll be seeing th' Earl an' what he looks like, an' that'll be something."

Nola laughed, but she felt very much the same.

She could not help feeling, however, if only she were doing this for William, how different it would be.

Yet William was dead and the Cousin who was too late in getting to Khartoum was in his place.

"How could this happen?" Nola asked despairingly.

But it had, and there was nothing she could do about it.

On Friday morning the Hall looked entirely different to what it had for the last two years.

Men from the village had come to clean the windows on the outside.

The footmen, inexperienced though they were, helped to polish the floors.

The Kitchen was abuzz with help from Mrs. Newman, who had cooked for the last ten years of the 5th Earl's life.

She was a good cook, Nola knew, as long as she had enough help.

She was getting old and found it hard to bend down.

Nola had provided her with two girls from the village.

She found others in another village, having been told they were very keen on cooking.

They were certainly eager to leave their present employment, where they were just general servants, to cook at the Hall.

Their employers, however, protested vigorously at being left at a moment's notice.

It took all Nola's tact and a certain amount of pleading to make the Doctor's wife and an elderly widow understand there was a crisis.

Also, whether they liked it or not, the Earl of Hallington's need was greater than theirs.

She only hoped when she looked round the Hall on Friday morning that the Earl would appreciate what they had done for him.

It had been a Herculean task.

She thought that Mrs. Chambers and the Newmans all deserved a medal.

She had an uncomfortable feeling, however, that the new Earl, being a bachelor, would have no idea what a commotion he had caused.

At the same time, he was a Ling.

'No-one,' Nola thought, 'could have been more charming and more understanding about everything than William.'

"Oh, why did he have to die in Khartoum?" she asked as she passed the Church, where a memorial had been erected to him.

His body had not come home to be buried in the family vault as was usual.

Instead, his Father had erected a beautiful carved memorial which stood in the Chancel.

'It might,' Nola thought, 'be admired now and for all the generations to follow, but that does not give them back William.'

Because he had been adventurous and because he was idealistic, she was quite certain he had enjoyed being with General Gordon.

He might even have relished the fight against overwhelming odds in which they had been finally defeated.

After leaving the Big House, she went back to the Vicarage.

It seemed small and empty without her Father.

She knew practically everyone in the village would be standing at the Lodge gates to see the Earl when he and his party arrived.

The older inhabitants would be peeping through the windows for a glimpse of his carriage as it drove past.

Nola lifted her legs on to the sofa and opened a book she was reading.

She did not get very far with it, as she kept thinking over what had happened this last year.

She was wondering now whether whenever she wished she would be able to go in and out of the Hall?

Whether she would be able to ride in the Park, as she had since a child?

Also, to enjoy, as her Father had once said laughingly, "the best crumbs were from a rich man's table."

That meant, of course, the peaches, the first strawberries, and all the other fruits as they ripened, besides what came from the Home Farm.

These delicacies had carried on as they always had done, right up to this moment.

It was only now that Nola was beginning to wonder whether the new Earl would make changes.

It would be at least polite to ask him if he wished such generosity to continue.

"Why, oh why, did this have to happen?" she asked the Fates.

She found it hard to believe, as her Father often said, that "God knew best."

The following morning, as usual, Mrs. Kettle came to work.

Nola knew as soon as she walked in with an unmistakeable glint in her eye, that she had a lot to say.

In fact, she never drew a breath as she cleaned out the fireplace.

Although Nola tried to escape, Mrs. Kettle kept on talking.

However, she told Nola some things she wanted to hear, one of them being that the new Earl was very good-looking.

She could not help thinking it would have been surprising if he had not been.

The late Earl had been a very handsome man, his wife a great beauty, and William was the best-looking young man Nola had ever seen.

When she looked at the pictures which hung on the walls at the Big House, she thought that the Lings, whether they were male or female, had extraordinarily good looks.

"Perhaps all we have heard about the Earl is wrong," she told herself, "and when he sees the Hall he will want to settle down and look after his big Estate."

She could not help feeling, however, that not all that Mrs. Kettle had told her about the party last night could be exaggerated.

Of course the local people would be surprised if the Earl's guests wore very low gowns.

Nola saw the pictures of London Beauties in the magazines wearing very *décolleté* evening dresses.

What did seem a little strange was that they stayed so long in the Dining-Room.

That meant that the Earl, being unmarried, did not understand that if he stayed up late, the whole household must do the same.

However old Newman might be, he would not be able to go to bed until all the silver had been put back in the safe and the door locked.

The china and glass must also be washed and put away.

The footmen helping him were country boys and they would undoubtedly be yawning their heads off.

'Perhaps this will happen only once,' she thought optimistically.

But at the same time she was worried.

She had always felt as if in some way Hallington Hall belonged to her and her Father as well as to the Ling family.

They had been so close for so many years.

She could hardly believe at this moment that it would be incorrect to walk into the Hall without being invited.

'There will be no-one to tell him about us,' she thought, 'and therefore I must just wait until Papa comes home. Then, of course, he will call on the Earl and ask him if there is anything he can do for him.'

She knew if she was truthful that she, too, wanted to see him.

Even though she was unfairly prejudiced against Rollo because he did not, with the Relief Force, reach Khartoum in time, she still wanted to make his acquaintance.

She often walked to the end of the garden and into the Park.

The gate was usually open because she would ride through it.

Moving under the great oak trees, where the spotted deer were, she would first reach the lake.

Then she would see the orchard on the other side of it.

In the Spring the blossoms on the pear, plum, and almond trees were breathtakingly beautiful.

When Nola moved beneath them, she felt she stepped into another world, which was, in fact, the world of her dreams.

The same thing happened when she rode in the woods, which she did nearly every morning.

There were a few gamekeepers left, and they were very old.

She could, therefore, ride for hours in the woods without seeing a soul.

It was only she who observed the rabbits rustling in the undergrowth, the squirrels climbing trees, and the birds singing as they fluttered through the branches.

In the centre of woods there was a mystical pool.

In the Spring it was surrounded with golden kingcups.

As a child she believed the nymphs lived in it and could be seen only in the moonlight.

"Was it possible," Nola asked now, "that the woods would be no longer mine, as they had been for so many years?"

Then she told herself hopefully that even if he appeared to be enjoying himself, the Earl would doubtless go back to the gaiety and frivolities of London.

Once he had gone, everything would be the same as it had always been.

Nola picked up her book and was just starting to read, when she heard a tap on the front-door.

She thought that by now Mrs. Kettle would have left for home.

Her old Nanny, who lived in the Vicarage with her, would be having a little snooze after luncheon.

She always declared indignantly that she did nothing of the sort.

She would sit down with her sewing in the window of the room that had once been the nursery.

After a few minutes, her eyes would close and she would fall asleep.

Nola had learned never to surprise her.

She would fumble with the door before she opened it, or else call out, "Nanny, Nanny" as she went up the stairs.

This meant that by the time she had entered the nursery, Nanny would have a needle in her hand.

Alternatively, she would be crocheting away at the lace she still made which ornamented the sheets and pillowcases in the Vicarage.

Knowing there was no-one else but herself to open the door, Nola got up from the sofa.

She crossed the small hall and opened the door, which was unlocked.

Outside, she was surprised to see Betsy.

She was one of the girls Nola had persuaded to come to the Hall to help Mrs. Chambers.

She was a little older than the others, being over seventeen and quite pretty except that she was slightly fat.

"Good afternoon, Betsy," Nola said.

She was thinking as she spoke that Betsy must have brought her a message from Mrs. Chambers.

"Can Oi have a word with yer, Miss Nola?" Betsy asked.

"Yes, of course," Nola answered.

She was slightly surprised and wondered what Betsy wanted to tell her.

She led the way into the Drawing-Room which her Mother had made so charming.

It had diamond-paned windows looking out over a rose garden.

Nola sat down on the sofa where she had been lying, and indicated an armchair next to it.

"Sit down, Betsy," she said. "Is everything all right up at the Hall?"

"Yes, Miss Nola, but us were run off our feet last night when th' ladies arrived."

"I can understand that," Nola said, "but I expect some of them brought their ladies'-maids."

"All six of 'em, Miss, but th' ladies'-maids be more difficult than they was."

Nola's eyes twinkled, but she did not say anything, and Betsy went on:

"Asking for this, an' asking for that, an' ever so snooty when us couldn't give 'em what they wanted."

"I expect being from London, they do not like coming to the country," Nola said.

"That be th' truth, Miss, ever so rude one or two were about us."

"But I do not expect you wanted to see me

17

about the ladies' maids," Nola said. "Tell me what you want."

"Well, it be like this, Miss, somethin' has happened an' Oi don't know what to do about it an' there be no-one Oi can ask 'cept you, although Oi would have gone to the Vicar if he'd been here."

Nola was surprised.

At the same time, she knew that Betsy and a number of the other boys and girls in the village had deep respect for her Father.

If anything was wrong, they went to him for advice rather than to their own Fathers and Mothers.

"As Papa is not here, Betsy, of course I will take his place," Nola said.

Again there was silence.

Betsy was twisting her fingers together.

Then she said:

"Mrs. Chambers says Oi can slip off home this mornin' 'cause as you knows, Mother's just had another baby an' her do need a bit o' help to get th' fire going."

"Yes, of course," Nola agreed.

"Well, Oi does what was wanted," Betsy said, "an' was coming back through th' Park, walking 'tween th' trees which makes it a short cut from th' village, when a man speaks to me."

"A man?" Nola said in surprise. "Who was he?"

"A Stranger, Miss Nola. Oi've never seen 'im before, an' a gentleman too."

Nola did not ask any questions, but waited, and Betsy went on:

"He said somethin' so strange to me, an' Oi don't know what t' do about it."

"What did he say?" Nola asked.

Betsy looked uncomfortable and twisted her fingers again.

Nola could not believe that the man, if he was a gentleman, would have made any advances to Betsy.

Although she was quite a pleasant-looking girl, she was very countrified.

"What 'e asked me," Betsy went on in a low voice, "was if Oi was one of th' housemaids from up at th' Big House. Oi told him I were, an' then 'e said that perhaps Oi'd like to earn a little money as 'e didn't expect they paid me much for what Oi does."

"How could you do that?" Nola enquired.

She thought this was an extraordinary conversation for a Stranger to be having with Betsy.

"This gentleman says to me," Betsy went on:

" 'Yer knows th' Earl, o' course, who came down last night?'

"Oi said yes, 'nd that Oi'd seen 'Is Lordship.

" 'And yer knows where 'e sleeps?' the Stranger enquired.

"Oi said:

" ' 'E sleeps in th' Master Suite'.

" 'Oi thought yer'd say that,' th' Stranger says."

Nola was listening, bewildered.

She could not understand what all this had to do with a strange man.

She was also aware that Betsy was very embarrassed.

Still twisting her fingers, she said:

"Then 'e says to me:

" 'Yer look to me a clever girl, an' when everyone has gone t'bed and yer find that th' Earl, yer Master, has moved from 'is bedroom into the one next to it, Oi wants yer to come an' tell me.' "

Nola gave a little gasp, and Betsy continued:

"Oi says to 'im, Oi says:

" 'Why should Oi do that?'

"An' he says to me, 'e says:

" 'Ye do as Oi tell yer and Oi'll give yer twenty pounds an' that be more than yer'll earn in a whole year. It'll be all yours to spend as yer like.' "

Nola opened her mouth to say something, but Betsy went on:

" 'E says:

" 'There's a staircase not far from th' Master Suite an' at th' bottom of it there be a door into th' garden. Oi'll be waiting there after 'Is Lordship's gone up to bed, an' yer come down very quietly an' let me in. Do yer understand?' "

There was a pause.

"Oi says to 'im." Betsy said:

" 'What do yer want to come in for?'

"An' 'e says:

" 'That be my business. Oi'll give you twenty pounds an' you can run back to yer bed an' go to sleep.' "

"I have never heard of anything so extraordinary," Nola exclaimed.

"That's what Oi thinks, Miss," Betsy agreed. "An' now Oi'm asking yer what do Oi do? 'Cause there be one more thing 'e says to me, an' that Oi haven't forgotten."

"What is it?" Nola asked.

" 'E says all nasty like:

" 'Say one word o' this to anyone in th' house or to th' Earl an' I'll cut yer tongue out. Yer can be quite sure o' that.'

"Oi'm frighted, Miss Nola, real frighted Oi am. Not 'cause Oi'm telling you, 'cause Oi knows yer'll not tell on me, but 'cause if Oi don't do what 'e says, 'e might cut me tongue out anyway."

There was no doubt that Betsy was frightened.

Now she was speaking in a voice different to the one she had used previously.

There was undoubtedly a note of fear in it.

It seemed to Nola an impossible story.

If it had been told by anyone other than Betsy, she would have thought it was a joke.

Betsy was a solid and very sensible girl.

She had been both baptised and confirmed by the Vicar.

He had always said when the children were in Church that he could rely on Betsy to keep the little ones in order.

Nola knew there were other girls who would have taken the money because it was such a large sum and not asked any questions.

It was like Betsy to come to the Vicar, and because he was not there, to come to her to ask what she should do.

It took Nola a second or two to decide what her answer should be.

Then she said very quietly:

"Now, listen to me, Betsy, I want you to do exactly what I tell you."

Betsy looked at her apprehensively.

"Yer don't think th' gentleman 'll hurt me, Miss Nola?"

"No-one will hurt you, Betsy. You were quite right to come to me, and, of course, you would have gone to my Father if he had been here."

"Oi thinks th' Vicar would say it be wrong o' me if Oi took money from a Stranger," Betsy said, "but as yer know, Miss Nola, Oi could do with twenty pounds. Oi would see my Mother

21

had a holiday which be what her needs after having a baby."

"That would be very kind of you," Nola said. "At the same time, you are employed by the Earl, and your loyalty, of course, is to him."

"Oi thinks yer would say that, Miss Nola," Betsy answered. "But what shall Oi do if th' gentleman gets nasty? An' nasty 'e'll be if 'e waits outside th' garden door an' there be no-one to open it for 'im."

Nola felt she could almost see what was working rather slowly in Betsy's mind.

Then she said quietly:

"You were absolutely right to come here and tell me what has happened. What I am going to do is to find out about this man and why he should want you to open the door. Only then can I give you an answer. Until then I know you will say nothing to anyone—no-one at all. Just go back to the Hall and do what Mrs. Chambers tells you."

"Tell me what Oi'm to do afore tonight comes, Miss Nola," Betsy pleaded. "Oi'll not be able t' sleep a wink, an' that's a fact. Oi'll be thinking about th' gentleman at th' door being very angry if 'e waits and waits and no-one comes."

"I understand all that," Nola said, "I think you have been very brave and have acted exactly in the way you should in coming here to me. Now, hurry back to the Hall and do not worry. I promise I will get in touch with you in the shortest time possible."

Betsy got up.

"Thank yer, Miss Nola," she said, "Oi'd better hurry 'cause Mrs. Chambers said Oi mustn't be long."

"Then hurry," Nola said, smiling, "and do not worry."

Betsy moved across the room.

Nola heard her go out through the front-door, shutting it behind her.

She then put her hand up to her forehead.

If only her Father were home, everything would be quite different.

But she knew, whether she wanted to or not, she now had to meet the Earl.

She could not help thinking it would be in the most unfortunate circumstances.

chapter two

AFTER Betsy had left, Nola pondered for a long time about when it would be best for her to go up to the Hall.

She thought it was likely that the Earl was either riding or in the garden before luncheon.

She therefore decided she would call early in the afternoon.

It must be before he and his party had set out on some other expedition.

She could only wish over and over again that her Father were there.

He would manage everything far better than she could.

At the same time, it was impossible for her to leave Betsy in such a predicament.

Besides, although she did not quite understand, the Stranger was obviously threatening the Earl in some way.

As she knew the house so well, she was aware the main guests would be sleeping in the same corridor as the Master Suite.

Mrs. Chambers would know who was sleeping in the next room to the Earl.

But if she asked questions, Mrs. Chambers

might be suspicious that she had a reason for them.

On one thing Nola was determined.

That was, if possible, that no-one would know that Betsy had been threatened by this strange man, whoever he might be.

Nanny had prepared luncheon for Nola.

She was very talkative about what she had heard from Mrs. Kettle about "the goings-on" up at the Big House.

"I'm sure your Father will not approve of what is happening," Nanny said, "and his late Lordship would turn in his grave."

Nola made no comment.

She felt everything had been said before.

She was also quite certain she would hear the same story again and again from everyone she met in the village.

When her luncheon, and it was a very light one, was over, she went to the stables.

She wanted *Sunbeam*, her own horse, which she had owned for some years.

She was allowed to ride all the horses which belonged to the Earl.

It therefore seemed an unnecessary extravagance for her and her Father to have more than one horse each.

These were kept at the Vicarage in case they were needed in an emergency.

Now Nola began to wonder, if she could not ride the horses at the Hall, whether her Father would be prepared to fill up his own stable.

It was something they had not bothered to do ever since she could remember.

When her Mother had been alive, there had been two carriage horses to take her driving whenever she wished to do so.

Again, if she had a long distance to go, the

horses at the Hall were faster and stronger.

What was more, the old Earl had liked her to use them.

"I enjoy seeing a pretty woman in an open carriage," he had said once. "There is something very feminine and attractive about it."

"Especially when the carriage is as good as yours," Nola's Mother had replied, "and the horses are as well-bred."

The Earl had laughed and said:

"I will come and take you driving tomorrow afternoon and we will decide who has the best pedigree—you, me, or my horses."

Nola thought of that and so many other things that had happened in the past.

She felt an ache in her heart.

"Why, oh, why, did everything have to be upset, when we were so happy?" she asked.

Once again she felt like crying because there was a stranger in William's place.

The old groom who had been with her Father for fifteen years saddled *Sunbeam* for her.

She rode across the Park as she had always done, under the oak trees and down towards the lake.

The kingcups were in bloom and the golden irises just showing their petals.

She knew that in the garden at the Hall the lilac would be coming into blossom.

In the orchard the pink and white blossoms on the fruit trees would in a week or so be breathtaking.

It was all so lovely and so familiar.

Nola was conscious of feeling a cold lump inside her breast because she had to meet the new Earl.

When she reached the Big House, she went straight to the stables.

Groves, the Head Groom, hurried out to greet her.

"Afternoon, Miss Nola," she said, "Oi was a-wondering when we'd see you."

"I did not intend to come today," Nola answered, "but I have a message for His Lordship. He has not gone out, has he?"

"Not to my knowledge," the Head Groom replied, "nor has 'e been to see th' horses."

Nola was surprised.

She somehow thought the Earl would have done that before he went round the house.

The stables had been the pride and joy of the late Earl and the delight of William's heart.

When he came home from school or University, the first thing he always did was to run to the stables and see the horses.

Of course he had his favourites.

They had been brushed and groomed until they were smarter, as his Father would say, "than any horse you will see in Rotten Row."

The groom took *Sunbeam* into a stall and Nola walked into the house by the back door.

Because she knew her way so well, there was no point in going round to the front.

After passing the pantry and the Dining-Room, she reached the Hall.

As Nola expected, Newman was there, having finished serving luncheon.

His old eyes lit up as he saw her.

"I want to see His Lordship alone," she said, "can you arrange it?"

"Yes, o' course, Miss Nola," Newman replied. "He be in th' Drawing-Room now with his guests. You go into the Ante-Room and I'll tell him where you are."

"Thank you," Nola said.

She crossed the hall and did not wait for Newman to open the door of the Ante-Room for her.

It was an attractive room which was next to the Drawing-Room and used only when they had very large parties.

If there were a number of guests staying in the house, it was a convenient place for them to write their letters.

The older guests would often have a quiet snooze there, where no-one was likely to disturb them.

Because Nola was feeling nervous, she did not sit down.

She walked across the room to the window and looked out into the garden.

It was looking very lovely.

The golden daffodils under the trees made a yellow carpet, and the tulips glowed crimson in some of the flower beds.

Also, as she had thought as she was riding here, the lilacs and syringas were coming into bloom.

She stood at the window feeling the sunshine and a touch of the breeze on her cheeks.

Then she was aware that she could hear voices through the open window of the Drawing-Room.

The Earl and his guests were talking rather loudly and laughing.

She could hear Newman say in his deep voice:

"Miss Brackley has called, M' Lord, and would like a word with you alone."

"Miss Brackley?" a man's voice questioned.

"Yes, My Lord. Miss Nola be the Vicar's daughter."

"I suppose I had better see her."

The sentence was spoken reluctantly.

Then another man's voice said much louder:

"Shut up your pockets, Rollo, you can be certain you will be asked to support some charity or other.''

The man who had spoken first laughed, and Nola knew it was the Earl.

"I suspect," he said, "it is the almshouses, the pensioners, or else the Church tower has fallen down."

There was a roar of laughter at this.

Nola realised for the first time that she was eavesdropping and moved away from the window.

As she waited for the door of the Ante-Room to open, she felt her anger rise within her.

It added to her dislike of the new Earl.

It was quite some minutes before the door opened.

She wondered for a moment if perhaps the Earl had refused to see her.

Then Newman said gravely.

"His Lordship, Miss Nola."

For a second it was difficult for Nola to look at him.

When she did so, she knew she had been right in thinking he would be good-looking.

He was also taller than she had expected.

As he walked towards her, she had to admit that he was typical of how the Ling men had looked all down the centuries.

"How do you do, Miss Brackley," the Earl said as he reached her.

"I am sorry to trouble you," Nola answered. "But something rather serious has occurred."

The Earl gave a sigh.

"Has the Church collapsed or the organ ceased to function?" he enquired.

Nola felt he was laughing at her, and she hated him for doing so.

"It is nothing like that," she said, "it is something which concerns you personally."

The Earl raised his eyebrows.

Then, as if he suddenly realised they were standing facing each other, he said:

"Perhaps, Miss Brackley, you would like to sit down and tell me what is troubling you. But I am afraid I cannot spare long, as I have to be with my guests."

"I am aware of that," Nola said, "and I assure Your Lordship that I would not have come to you if it had not been a matter of importance."

She saw by the expression on the Earl's face that he was quite convinced that whatever she had to say would not be of importance to him.

He settled himself in one of the comfortable chairs in front of the fireplace and crossed his legs.

Nola sat down on the edge of the sofa.

She was trying to find words in which to explain why she had come, and was finding it extremely difficult.

"Well, what is it?" the Earl said after several seconds had passed.

"This morning, just before luncheon," Nola replied, "one of the girls, who your Housekeeper, Mrs. Chambers, has engaged as a housemaid, came to see me with a very extraordinary story which I think you will find hard to believe."

The Earl did not reply.

She thought there was a somewhat cynical twist to his lips as she went on:

"Betsy, for that is the girl's name, told me that she had been allowed to slip home this morning to help her Mother, who has just had a baby."

The Earl looked at the clock on the mantlepiece.

Nola was aware he was wondering how this could possibly concern him.

Hurrying because she knew he was impatient, she went on quickly:

"On her way back from the village, Betsy was confronted by a Stranger who she thought was a gentleman. He asked her if she was a housemaid here, and when she told him she was, he asked her if she knew where you slept."

Now Nola was aware she had at last aroused a little attention from the Earl.

He turned his head to look at her in surprise.

Before he could ask any questions, she went on:

"Betsy said that yes, it was in the Master Suite, and the Stranger said he would give her twenty pounds if tonight, when she was aware you had moved into another bedroom, she would come downstairs and open the garden door and let him in."

The Earl sat bolt upright in his chair.

"Are you telling me the truth, Miss Brackley," he said, "or is this some strange joke?"

"I assure Your Lordship this is no joke," Nola said coldly, "and you should be glad that Betsy was brave enough to come and tell me what had occurred rather than just obey the Stranger's instructions which he gave her with a threat that has made her very frightened."

"What sort of threat?" the Earl asked.

"He told her in a manner that terrified her that if she said anything in the house or to you of what he had suggested, he would 'cut her tongue out.'"

Because it sounded so extraordinary, Nola dropped her voice when she said the last words.

She was aware as she did so that the Earl was staring at her in sheer astonishment.

There was a silence, and then he said:

"You are quite sure it is true and the young

woman who told it to you has not invented the whole thing."

"I hardly think any village girl would invent such a fantastic story," Nola said. "I have known Betsy ever since I have lived here. She is a well-behaved girl from a decent family of whom my Father has always approved."

The Earl got up from his chair and walked across the room.

As she had done, he stood at the window, looking out into the garden.

Then he came back to stand in front of the fireplace.

"Do you think this young woman will talk to other people?" he asked.

"She came to my Father because everyone in the village takes their problems to him. It is only because he is away at the moment that she told me what had happened. I am quite certain she will not speak to anyone else."

The Earl did not speak, and she knew he was thinking hard.

Then he said somewhat harshly:

"I suppose you understand exactly what is implied by all of this?"

Nola looked up at him wide-eyed.

"I have really not the slightest idea," she said. "It seems to me an extraordinary request. Why should he want to pay so much money unless it is to get into the house and rob you?"

"It is rather more complicated than that," the Earl said.

The way he spoke made Nola look at him in surprise.

When he did not continue, she said a little nervously:

"What do you want me to do?"

"That is just what I have been thinking," the

Earl answered. "I should have thought, even though you are the Vicar's daughter, you would realise that what this Stranger intends is to catch me in what is known as a 'compromising position.'"

Nola's eyes seemed to fill her whole face, and then she said:

"I . . . did not think . . . of that . . . and you mean it is blackmail?"

"No," the Earl said. "What this Stranger, and I think I know who he is, intends, is, if he is let into the house, he will bring a detective with him. I will then find myself fighting a duel with a very experienced opponent."

"A duel!" Nola gasped. "I thought they were forbidden."

"They take place in London occasionally and continually on the Continent," the Earl replied.

Nola tried to grasp what he was saying.

Then, as the Earl did not continue, she said:

"Surely if I tell Betsy . . . not to open . . . the door . . . you will not be . . . involved. But I am afraid she will still be . . . frightened that the man might . . . avenge himself on . . . her as he has . . . threatened . . . to do."

The Earl walked across the room and back again, then he said:

"I have a better idea than that. As I have already told you, I think I am aware of who this man is, and to save further threats to your young *protégée*, the sooner I confront him the better."

"I . . . do not . . . understand," Nola said.

"It is quite simple," the Earl replied. "The girl lets in the Stranger, who I am quite certain will be accompanied by a detective. She shows him up to the room next to mine, where I will be waiting for them."

"If anything went . . . wrong perhaps . . . the

Stranger will still take his ... revenge on ... Betsy," Nola said.

"If that perturbs you, Miss Brackley," the Earl replied, "it might be easier for you to take her place."

Nola stared at him as if she could not believe what he had just said.

He went on, planning out every detail.

"You can be a housemaid here just for tonight. Open the door to the man who is waiting outside. He will follow you up the stairs and doubtless give you the twenty pounds he promised."

He said the last words almost as if he were laughing.

Nola thought there was a glint in his eye, as if he were now almost enjoying the situation.

"Surely I am not asking too much of you?" he went on. "After all, an extra housemaid just for one night need not be a great surprise to anyone."

Now Nola thought he was insulting her, and she said:

"As I was responsible for finding the house-maids for Mrs. Chambers and, as it happens, the footmen for Newman, I think they would be considerably surprised and embarrassed if I suddenly joined them in the way Your Lordship suggests."

The Earl looked at her as if he saw her for the first time.

Then he said quickly:

"I have no wish to be insulting, Miss Brackley. Of course I had no idea you were so deeply involved in my household."

"Your Lordship has obviously not been told," Nola said coldly, "that after the Earl died and William was killed, there was no-one to give any orders. My Father and your Manager, Mr. Mansfield, did what they thought was best for the house and the Estate."

She drew in a breath before she continued:

"When you told us last Tuesday you were arriving on Friday, there was only a skeleton staff of very old servants in the house. The whole place had to be cleaned and got ready with the minimum amount of time in which to do it."

The Earl was looking at her in astonishment, and he said:

"Of course I had no idea the house had not continued to function after the Earl's death as it always had."

"You must be aware," Nola said sharply, "that over a year has passed since Your Lordship inherited the title."

"My only excuse," the Earl replied, "although I do not know why I should make one, was that I was sent back to England wounded. I was running a high temperature and only half-conscious until I found myself in a London hospital."

He hesitated, as if it were an effort to go on:

"Even then it was several weeks before I heard that the Earl was dead, and also my Cousin William. I never even in my wildest dreams imagined that I would become the Earl of Hallington."

Because he spoke so sincerely, Nola felt she had judged him unfairly, and she said quickly:

"We did our best in the short time we had, and I hope Your Lordship is satisfied."

"Very satisfied," the Earl said. "What I did not expect was the unpleasant news you have just brought me."

Nola made a little helpless gesture with her hands.

"I had to tell you," she said

"Yes, of course you did," he agreed. "Now I will ask you, Miss Brackley, if you will help me in a different manner to what I suggested before."

"I would like to help you," Nola replied, "but

I am most concerned about Betsy. We have never had threats, or, for that matter, scandal here in this lovely house."

"I can only hope it is something that will not happen again," the Earl said. "But we are still faced with an enemy who wishes to involve me in a scandal which will be not only vulgar and unpleasant, but also dangerous."

"You mean if it comes to a duel, you might be killed." Nola said.

"It is extremely likely," the Earl said, "because the man who will challenge me has already killed two opponents in Italy."

"Then, please, you must do something about it." Nola begged. "The Ling family has always been very proud, and I could not bear their name to be dragged in the dust."

"That is exactly what it will be," the Earl said, "if this so-called Stranger has his way."

"Please explain it to me, because I do not understand," Nola said.

The Earl sat down again in the seat he had previously vacated.

"I have been well aware that I have a bitter enemy," he said quietly, "and although I could never believe it, I have heard that he has boasted at the Club that he would get rid of me within a very short time and take my place."

Now Nola gave a sudden start.

She knew or thought she must know who the Stranger and the enemy of the Earl was.

Of course it was his Cousin Basil, who had already tried to prove he was the rightful successor to the 5th Earl.

As if he could read her thoughts, the Earl said:

"You are quite right, Miss Brackley, my Cousin Basil is determined to be rid of me, and I have to admit that this would have been quite a clever scheme if he had been able to bring it off."

"But why, and how?" Nola asked in a bewildered little voice.

"I have staying with me here," the Earl said, "the *Contessa* di Silvani, whose husband is attached to the Italian Embassy. She is very beautiful—one of the most beautiful women London has ever seen. Not surprisingly, her husband, the *Conte*, is extremely jealous. He is also the most notable duelling shot in the whole of Italy."

"So your Cousin Basil thought the *Conte* would challenge you to a duel and kill you," Nola murmured.

"Exactly," the Earl said, "that is why I am quite certain of the reason the Stranger wants to be let in tonight. He will have with him a detective who, on the *Conte's* instructions, is watching his wife while he is away in Rome."

"Then of course you must be very careful," Nola murmured.

"That is what I intend to be, with your help," the Earl said. "I think it would be a great mistake, and I am sure you agree, to let the housemaid, who you say is only a young girl, to be any further involved in this plot."

Nola nodded, and he continued:

"I will therefore ask you, Miss Brackley, if you will be kind enough to dine with me here tonight? As I understand your Father is away, it would be much more convenient if you stayed the night rather than return home after dinner."

Nola was listening to him wide-eyed, and he said:

"If you slip downstairs in the evening and let in my Cousin and the detective, it is doubtful if he will realise in the dark that you are not the girl to whom he offered twenty pounds. All you have to do is to bring them up to the landing, which will be in semi-darkness, and indicate the room next to mine."

Having finished, the Earl waited and looked enquiringly at Nola.

"I . . . suppose I . . . could do . . . that," she said, "if it will . . . save you—and . . . of course Betsy—from . . . being involved."

"It will save us both," the Earl said, "and as you seem to know this house so well, perhaps you could think of some reason why the *Contessa* di Silvani should be moved from the room next to mine, where she spent last night, into another bedroom presumably in the same corridor."

Nola smiled.

"You have two alternatives," she said. "Fires smoke if you push something a little way up the chimney, and several years ago we did have a little trouble with a rat or mouse which died beneath the floorboards. There was an exceedingly unpleasant smell before it was removed."

The Earl laughed.

It was a spontaneous sound and seemed for the moment to break the tension which Nola had felt ever since he had come into the room.

"I think it is still cold at night," he said after a moment, "so we will have a smoking fire. I will attend to it just before the ladies come up to dress for dinner."

Because she felt the conversation was at an end, Nola rose to her feet.

"Do you really . . . wish me to take . . . part in this . . . drama?" she said hesitatingly.

"The truth is, Miss Brackley," the Earl replied, "I cannot do it without you. I think you will agree that it is better to give my Cousin a real sharp shock and send him back to London in an ignominious manner than to have him prowling around the outside of the house picking up what else he can find to discredit me."

"Yes, I think you are right," Nola agreed.

"Therefore, you will honour me by being my guest at dinner?" the Earl said.

"If you want me," Nola replied.

"I will leave Betsy in your hands," the Earl went on as if he were still thinking of his plan, "and perhaps you would tell my Housekeeper that you will be staying here tonight."

"Yes, I will tell her," Nola said, "and I will also tell Betsy that there is no need for her to worry, and that she is not required to do anything or even think about what happened again."

"I doubt if she will be able to do that," the Earl said with an unexpected smile, "and I also think, Miss Brackley, that she will be very disappointed to lose the twenty pounds my Cousin so generously offered her."

His eyes were twinkling as he added:

"At least it was less than thirty pieces of silver."

He put his hand in the inside pocket of his coat and drew out a notecase.

"I think to conclude the situation properly, Betsy should have her twenty pounds," he said.

He drew a bill out of his case and held it out towards Nola.

"I think . . . that is a . . . mistake," she said.

"Nonsense," the Earl replied. "Having been very poor myself, I know what it means to be offered a large sum of money and then have it snatched away. Give the girl the twenty pounds and tell her to keep her mouth shut. Nothing can be said in London, at any rate, if my Cousin does not find me in the incriminating circumstances he expects."

"You are quite . . . certain it is . . . your Cousin?" Nola asked.

"There is no-one else who would benefit by my death," the Earl said, "and I can assure you, Miss Brackley, having been of no consequence for a great number of years, I find it strange and, if you like, a little intimidating, to know now how much more valuable I am dead than alive."

"You must not talk like that," Nola said. "Of course it is very wicked of your Cousin to try to injure you."

"It is not a question of injury," the Earl said quietly. "He will be disposing of me in a way for which he will not be hanged."

"I cannot believe it!" Nola cried. "How can this conversation be taking place here in Hallington Hall, where everything has always been so quiet and so peaceful."

There was a little throb in her voice as she said the last word, and the Earl said:

"That is what we must try and make it in the future, and I admit that I was wrong in not deciding to do that until now."

Nola looked at him in surprise, and then she said:

"Can I ask you to do something?"

"Yes, of course," the Earl said, "if it is not too unpleasant."

"I do not think you will find it so," Nola said. "But you can understand that, having been ignored for a year, everyone on your Estate, and you know it is a very large one, is longing to see you and wanting to meet you."

The Earl stared at her, and then he said:

"I had not thought of that, but of course I must go and call on them. You mean the farmers, and the people in the village and, naturally, the Vicar?"

"That is the right idea, and I am sure that is what Papa would have said to you if he were here. And if you will forgive me telling you, the first thing you should have done as a Ling would be to call on the stables."

"You mean there are horses here?" the Earl asked.

"Of course there are, and very fine ones too. The Earl was very particular that he drove only the very best carriage horses, and William was an exceptionally fine rider."

She thought the Earl looked excited.

Then he said, almost as if he were speaking to himself:

"I have never had a horse of my own, and this will certainly be a new experience."

"At the moment you own twenty-four in the stable," Nola said, "a number of mares out to grass, and some yearlings which will be at their best in a year's time."

"I can hardly believe it," the Earl said. "I do not know why, but this is something I never expected."

"Then you must certainly keep alive," Nola said, "and enjoy Hallington Hall, which to me is the most beautiful house in the world. It has everything that a Landlord could possibly require."

"Why did no-one tell me this was waiting for me?" the Earl asked.

"Perhaps it will be all the more exciting because it is a surprise," Nola said. "Now I will go and speak to Mrs. Chambers. Thank you, My Lord, for your invitation to stay the night."

"I hope by the time we meet again, Miss Brackley," the Earl said, "to know a great deal more about my possessions than I know at the moment."

Nola smiled at him and left the room.

The Earl did not follow her but went again to

the window to look out into the garden.

Once again he was not seeing the beauty of the stream and the shrubs and flowers.

He was realising he had been saved from what could undoubtedly have been an ignominious death by the daughter of a Vicar.

He was thinking how incredible it would seem to the party he had next door.

How they would laugh and jest about it if they knew the truth.

But he was aware that his Cousin Basil, in his insane desire to be rid of him, would have worked out every step he was taking.

He was determined to dispose of someone who stood between him and the Earldom.

The Earl had come down from London, travelling for the first time in his life in his own railway carriage attached to the train.

He had chosen, from among his friends, guests who he thought would make an amusing and riotous weekend.

They were friends who seemed to have appeared from nowhere when he was convalescent and had moved from the hospital into Ling House in Park Lane.

He had never asked himself whether they were the right sort of companions for someone of his importance to have.

He had only been so thrilled and delighted that he could afford to wine and dine them.

For the first time in his life he could give parties.

He was flattered, and in his own words "seduced," by the most beautiful women in London.

He had been enamoured of the *Contessa* di Silvani from the moment he saw her.

With her dark hair and flashing eyes which

held just a touch of green in them, she was irresistible.

To a young man who had never met anyone like her before, she was unbelievable.

The *Conte* had been called back to Rome for an important meeting.

It had seemed a marvellous opportunity to bring the *Contessa* to the country.

The Earl had made quite certain on his arrival that her bedroom was next to his.

Last night their fiery love-making had taken the thought of anything else out of his mind.

Now he knew he was walking a tightrope.

One slip would mean his utter and complete destruction.

"How can I have been such a fool," he asked himself, "not to be aware that Basil was watching me and was determined to kill me?"

chapter three

NOLA told Mrs. Chambers that she was going to stay the night.

Mrs. Chambers smiled her approval.

"That's how it should be, Miss Nola," she said. "It's a real pity that the Vicar couldn't be here when His Lordship arrived."

Nola could only agree, but she was in a hurry to get home.

"I must go and tell Nanny that I am coming here, and, of course, get her to pack my best dress."

Mrs. Chambers smiled. Then she said:

"You can hardly carry your best dress on a horse, Miss Nola. I suggest you ask someone from the stables to send a carriage for you and your luggage."

Nola laughed.

"There will not be as much as all that, but I think your idea is a good one, Mrs. Chambers, and perhaps I should arrive in grandeur."

Mrs. Chambers laughed.

Nola went towards the door of the Housekeeper's room, there they were talking, then paused.

"Do you know where Betsy is?" she enquired. "I want to ask her about her Mother and whether she requires anything in particular now that the baby is born."

"I hear she's doing very well," Mrs. Chambers said. "Your Mother, bless her heart, always gave the women somethin' special to build them up after they had a baby."

"I remember that," Nola replied.

"You'll find Betsy in th' linen room," Mrs. Chambers went on. "I told her to iron some face towels which were washed this morning."

"I will go and see her," Nola replied, "and I look forward to seeing you tonight."

"It'll be just like old times to have you dining at th' Hall," Mrs. Chambers said.

Nola hurried down the corridor to the linen room.

Betsy was there, and another of the girls from the village was with her.

Nola looked at her and then said:

"I want to speak to you a moment, Betsy."

She saw by the expression on Betsy's face that she was apprehensive.

She put down the iron and hurried to the door.

Nola drew her outside.

"You are not to worry any more," she said. "His Lordship has everything in hand and promises that the Stranger will not hurt you."

"Ye're quite sure of that, Miss Nola?" Betsy added.

"Quite sure," Nola replied, "and because His Lordship thought you were so brave and sensible, he has given you the twenty pounds you would have received from the Stranger."

She drew it from her pocket as she spoke.

Betsy stared at the note as if she could not believe her eyes.

"Oi hardly likes to take it, Miss, when Oi've done nothin' to earn it."

"You have earned it by doing exactly what I would have wanted you to do," Nola replied. "You came to me as you would have gone to my Father and also you have not spoken about this to anyone else."

"Oi gives yer my word, Miss," Betsy said, "and yer knows Oi'll not break it."

"Yes, I know that," Nola said. "And do not let anyone know you have so much money, because they will be curious and ask where it has come from."

She saw by the expression on Betsy's face that she had thought of this already.

The one good thing in the whole of this unpleasantness, Nola thought, was that Basil Ling had talked to Betsy.

Another girl might have been completely hysterical and not known what to do about it.

She let herself out of one of the side doors, which led to the stables.

She asked Groves, the Head Groom, if he would be kind enough to fetch her from the Vicarage before dinner.

"That'll be a pleasure, Miss Nola," he said, "Oi hopes tomorrow yer'll be riding some of our horses. *Mercury* has missed yer the last few mornings."

Mercury was a horse of which Nola was particularly fond.

She could not resist going to his stall and making a fuss of him.

He nuzzled against her.

As he did, she sent up a little prayer in her heart that she still might be able to ride him again.

The head Groom had *Sunbeam* ready for her and was holding him in the yard, when the Earl appeared with two other men.

Nola, who had not yet mounted, thought it was

only polite to wait until they had reached her.

She was aware that the two men with the Earl looked at her curiously.

"You will be meeting Miss Brackley at dinner tonight," he said.

Nola shook the two men by the hand, noting that one was called Lord Longdon and the other Sir Richard Cross.

Lord Longdon patted *Sunbeam* and said:

"You have a fine mount here, Miss Brackley. Is there a good fox-hunting pack in this part of the world?"

"There are two very good ones," Nola replied, "but they are not so fashionable as those in Leicestershire."

"Then you will have to bring them up to scratch, Rollo," Lord Longdon said laughingly.

"I am told I have some decent horses with which to do so," the Earl replied.

"That's what Oi've been waiting for yer to see, Yer Lordship," the Head Groom interposed, "an' Miss Nola'll tell yer there ain't a stable within one hundred miles of 'ere as could compete with any of 'em."

The Earl looked at Nola.

"I have a feeling," he said quietly, "that as well as seeing to my house before my arrival, you have also been concerned with my stables."

"How could I have been anything else," Nola replied, "when I have ridden the horses in it since I was in the cradle?"

The Earl laughed, and then Lord Longdon said:

"Come and show us which are the best and the fastest horses so that we shall have a chance of beating our host if he tries to race us."

Nola hesitated.

Then, as the Earl seemed willing, she went with the three men into the stables.

She knew that Groves was delighted to show off the horses.

Although her Father and Mr. Mansfield had cut down the staff everywhere else, they had left the Head Groom enough stable to keep the horses well-groomed and exercised.

As they went from stall to stall, she could see what the Earl was feeling by the expression on his face.

He was thrilled beyond words at finding himself unexpectedly an owner of really outstanding horseflesh.

They looked at every horse in the stables.

Groves then suggested he should show His Lordship those in the paddock.

"I think I should go home now," Nola said to the Earl. "I hope you do not mind, but I have asked Groves to send a carriage for me before dinner."

"No, of course you must be collected," the Earl replied.

"And as you are staying the night," Lord Longdon chipped in, "do not forget to pack your riding habit. I have a feeling that you would be a formidable opponent if I raced you before breakfast tomorrow morning."

Nola took in her breath sharply.

This was something she wanted above all things, but she was afraid the Earl might think she was pushing.

She looked at him apprehensively.

As if he knew what she was longing to do, he said: "But of course Miss Brackley must ride with us tomorrow morning. I have a suspicion that all our lady guests are Hyde Park trotters."

The men laughed at this, and Nola allowed Groves to help her into the saddle.

She had achieved, by a miracle, everything she wanted.

She had no wish to push her luck any further.

She rode away, looking, although she was not aware of it, very picturesque on *Sunbeam*.

As she did so, she was saying a silent prayer of gratitude that she could ride the horses in the stables at the Big House.

When she told Nanny where she was going tonight, the old woman said sharply:

"Quite right too! After all your Father had done for his house, his Estate, and, of course, them horses, I should expect His Lordship to be grateful—and very grateful at that."

"But you must understand, Nanny," Nola said, "there was no-one to tell him what Papa had done and it was very embarrassing having to more or less tell him myself."

Nanny was not listening.

She had opened the wardrobe in Nola's bedroom and was looking at it somewhat disparagingly.

"From what I hears from Mrs. Kettle," she said, "the ladies up at the Hall be looking like the Queen of Sheba, and that'll be more than you'll be with these gowns."

Nola had been thinking the same thing as she rode home.

She told herself, however, that it was no use trying to compete with women like the *Contessa*. She had been described as the most beautiful woman London had ever seen, and, of course, she would be the best-dressed.

Yet she could not help wishing that she had taken a little more trouble over her evening gowns.

There had been no parties at the Big House after the Earl was ill and then died.

The neighbours seemed inclined to forget her when they had house-parties.

She was sensible enough to realise than an unattached girl was always something of a liability.

Although occasionally she and her Father were asked out together, the invitations were few and far between.

Nanny suddenly gave an exclamation.

"I have an idea," she said, "and there's no reason to leave it mouldering in the cupboard with no-one to admire it."

"What are you talking about?" Nola enquired.

"The gown your Mother had specially for the Hunt Ball. Very lovely her looked in it, but t'was after that evening she was taken ill and never wore the gown again."

"I am not . . . certain that I want . . . to wear it," Nola began in a low voice.

"Now, that's just stuff and nonsense," Nanny said. "It's a beautiful gown which cost a great deal of money, and why should it waste away when the one person who'd want you to look smart tonight would be your Mother."

Nola knew this was sheer common sense.

Yet she was still a little reluctant to allow Nanny to go to her Mother's room and bring back the gown in question.

When she saw it, she remembered how beautiful her Mother had looked before she and her Father set off for the Ball.

Nola had not been asked because she was too young.

When her Mother had kissed her goodbye, she said:

"Next year, Darling, we will all go together. I know Papa and I will be very proud of you."

There had not been a next year for Nola, who was then in mourning.

Last year she knew that her Father would not want to go to the Ball at which he would so vividly remember her Mother.

Now, when she saw the gown, she knew whatever memories it might have, it was exactly what she needed tonight.

After all, she was sure it would be the smartest dinner-party to which she would ever be invited.

The gown that her Mother had chosen with a great deal of care was the blue of a forget-me-not.

It had just a touch of silver here and there in the frills and on the bodice.

It made the gown seem as if it shimmered with every movement.

Nola knew it had been the colour of her Mother's eyes.

Actually hers were the same, just as her hair was the same pale gold as her Mother's.

She thought when she was dressed that she was glad that her Father was not there tonight.

It would have hurt him to see her as a replica of the wife he had lost.

As if Nanny knew what she was thinking, she said:

"Now, just you enjoy yourself, Dearie, and remember all that you and your Father have done for His Lordship. If he were sensible enough to realise it, he'd be down on his knees thanking you."

As Nanny spoke, Nola found herself shivering.

There was another way and a very frightening one in which she had to help the Earl.

She could not help wondering as she drove up the Hall what would happen if things went wrong, if perhaps it was not his Cousin Basil who was his enemy, but someone else.

Then she thought it was almost impossible for anyone to have two such enemies.

She wondered what would happen after the Earl had told his Cousin what he thought of him.

Would Basil still persist in his intention to kill him?

"It cannot be true," Nola said aloud as the carriage moved up the drive. "Can anything so horrible be really happening here, where everyone has always been so happy?"

Quite suddenly she felt really afraid of what might occur tonight.

She wished she had not told the Earl of the problem Betsy had brought her.

Instead, she could have laughed it off as being something entirely ridiculous.

But she knew this would have been impossible.

It was undoubtedly the truth and therefore had to be faced.

She was worrying about the Earl and what would happen later in the evening.

Therefore, it did not strike her that arriving as a stranger amongst a number of people who were all close friends was actually an ordeal.

Newman met her in the hall and said:

"It's real nice to have you here, Miss Nola. Mrs. Newman has made your favourite pudding for dinner."

"How kind of her," Nola exclaimed. "Tell her I will come and see her tomorrow."

"Her'll be looking forward to that, Miss Nola," Newman said.

He gave the wrap which Nola had worn over her dress to a footman.

He carried it rather clumsily and put it down on one of the chairs in the hall.

Then Newman went ahead towards the Drawing-Room door.

As he opened it, Nola heard a burst of laughter from the end of the room.

For the first time she felt shy.

She had no idea how lovely she looked in the light of the Chandeliers.

After Newman had announced her, she moved slowly towards the fireplace, where the party had congregated.

The Earl had seen her only in her riding habit with her hair severely and tidily brushed back.

Now the light from the candles seemed to sparkle on Nola's fair, curly hair.

As it framed her small face, it was almost like a halo.

She had always had a very white skin which was not affected by the sun.

Because she was so young, she seemed to the men watching her to advance like the spirit of Spring.

The Earl quickly moved towards her.

"Good evening, Miss Brackley," he said, "I am so delighted to welcome you here into the house, which you know so much better than I do myself."

Nola gave a little laugh.

"I am sure that is the wrong thing to say," she replied, "but I have known it and loved it all my life."

"Who could ask for more?" Lord Longdon said.

He was a nice-looking man, a little bit older than the Earl and not so tall.

He had a somewhat flirtatious manner, which Nola found a little embarrassing.

He was sitting on one side of her at dinner.

At times he made her blush with his compliments and also feel a little out of her depth with the rest of his conversation.

The party at the Hall was very different to any party she had ever attended before.

It was not what anyone would have expected to find in the country.

The *Contessa* was exquisitely beautiful, there was no doubt about that.

At the same time, there was something exotic and sensuous about her which was very un-English.

It was with difficulty that Nola prevented herself from staring at her wide-eyed instead of trying to understand what she was saying.

The other ladies in the party were very much the same.

Their dresses were as *décolleté* as Mrs. Kettle had described them.

Their faces all had touches of rouge and powder on them.

Their conversation had, with practically every word, what the French called a *"double entendre."*

They certainly flirted with an expertise with the men on either side of them.

The *Contessa* flashed her eyes at the Earl and with every word she spoke made her lips seem to invite his kisses.

Nola was not exactly shocked.

She was, in fact, bewildered and at the same time fascinated.

This was a new world in which she was a complete stranger.

She realised by the time dinner had finished that the ladies present were married but staying with the Earl without their husbands.

The men with whom they seemed so familiar were, she thought, something very special in their lives at this particular moment.

Nola listened to the trills of laughter accompanied by glances from eyes which spoke more clearly than words.

She told herself it was like watching a play taking place on the stage while she consisted of the entire audience.

"You are very lovely," she heard Lord Longdon say in a low voice. "How is it possible you can be a Vicar's daughter?"

"Are there any particular rules as to how a Vicar's daughter should look?" Nola enquired.

"I cannot say I am very knowledgeable about them as a race," Lord Longdon replied, "but all the Vicar's daughters I have met previously have not looked like you."

Nola glanced round the table.

If these were the usual friends with whom he moved, they would certainly seem very strange to any Vicar's daughter like herself.

As dinner progressed, everyone seemed to drink a great deal of the excellent Champagne and the other wines which were served with the different courses.

Nola was worrying a little as to how the footmen would manage.

She was relieved to find that on the whole they waited quite well and did not make too many mistakes.

She was relieved when the dinner ended earlier than last night.

She thought it was because the Earl was aware of what they had to do when his guests had gone to bed.

Once or twice she caught him looking at her in a meaningful way.

Because she thought he was as nervous as she was, she gave him a reassuring little smile.

When the ladies, led by the *Contessa*, left the Dining-Room, Nola heard nearly every one of them say to the man who had been beside her:

"Now, do not be long."

Some even added:

"Otherwise I shall come and fetch you."

The *Contessa*, obviously used to the Continental ways, said to the Earl:

"Bring the Port or whatever it is you are drinking into the Drawing-Room."

She then lowered her voice, but Nola heard her quite clearly say:

"I want you with me."

It was spoken in a very seductive tone, in fact, so seductive that Nola found herself blushing.

She could not imagine her Mother speaking like that.

If this was the type of party the Earl preferred, then he was not likely to stay long in the country.

That could mean the house being shut up again and the Estate forgotten.

She found herself suddenly feeling dismayed and almost frightened.

What would happen to the village and to everything else if the Earl went back to London and was no longer interested?

Then, almost like a star shining in a dark sky, she remembered how thrilled he had been with the horses.

That was what would keep him here in this house, where be belonged.

The horses which filled the stables would be irresistible to even the most fastidious horseman.

Since they had left the Drawing-Room, the card tables had been laid out at one end of the room.

There was also a Roulette wheel which Nola had never seen before.

"I am not going to gamble tonight," she heard one of the Gentlemen say when they joined the Ladies. "I lost a packet last night. Hallington can afford it—I cannot."

The Earl, however, did not seem as if he wished to play cards.

Several of the women sat down at the Roulette table and held out their hands to the men who escorted them.

Nola for a moment did not understand what they were doing.

Then she saw they were asking for money with which to play.

She was quite sure this was another thing of which her Mother would disapprove.

When the Earl said to her:

"What do you want to do, Miss Brackley?" she answered quickly.

"I am afraid I have never gambled, although I can play Whist."

The Earl laughed.

"I think you would find that even more expensive than Roulette."

Nola looked surprised before she said:

"We are very . . . countrified . . . in Hallington."

"It would be a mistake to be anything else," the Earl replied.

He was about to add something, when the *Contessa* came up to him.

"I want to stake a great deal of money on number six," she said in her slightly broken accent. 'Give me everything you have in your pocket, Rollo, because I am sure I am in luck tonight."

The Earl pulled out a wad of notes which made Nola gasp.

Then she told herself angrily that he was throwing money away when there was a great deal which needed doing on the Estate.

The farmers needed money spent on their vehicles and on repairs.

In the village the pensioners had not had a rise for the last three years.

Food and everything else was more expensive than it had been before the Earl died.

How could the Earl give this Italian, just because she was beautiful, so much money?

It should be spent on people who really needed it.

Because she felt upset, Nola walked to the window.

She drew back the curtains a little so that she could look out at the moonlit garden.

The stars were like diamonds in the sky, and she thought nothing could be so lovely.

"You are very lovely too," she heard a voice say, and realised that Lord Longdon was standing beside her.

She gave him a quick glance and looked away again.

Because he was standing closer to her than was necessary, she felt embarrassed.

"Shall we go out in the garden?" he asked.

It struck Nola that she would much prefer to be in the garden.

She hated being in a room where money was thrown away unnecessarily by over-dressed exotic women.

Then she remembered the Stranger might be there, and said quickly:

"No . . . of course . . . not."

"Why not?" Lord Longdon enquired. "Are you afraid of me or afraid of your reputation?"

"Neither," Nola replied. "I am only hoping we shall not be too late in going to bed."

He looked at her in a way she did not understand.

Then he said in a somewhat dry tone:

"I think most of the party will be voting for an early night, so you will not be disappointed."

Nola looked at him.

She did not understand the expression in his eyes or the twist to his lips.

"I know you keep late hours in London," she said, "but here in the country we get up early, and that makes it a very long day."

"What I am looking for," Lord Longdon said, "is a very long night."

Again Nola did not understand.

The Earl came across the room to say to her:

"Are you quite sure, Miss Brackley, you do not want to play? I expect you have realised that at this sort of party if a woman wins, the gains are hers. But if she loses, someone gallantly pays up for her."

He looked at Lord Longdon in a rather pointed way as he spoke.

Then he added:

"Edie is complaining that she is already broke."

"It does not surprise me," Lord Longdon said.

He turned and walked towards the card table.

As Nola and the Earl were alone, she said to him:

"How soon do you think we should go upstairs?"

"About midnight," he replied, "not later, if I can help it."

He seemed about to say something more, when the *Contessa* called from the Roulette table:

"Rollo, Rollo, I want you."

The Earl went towards her obediently.

Nola, realising she was alone, slipped out of the room without anyone being aware of it.

She felt she had nothing in common with the women playing Roulette or the men gambling highly at the Bridge table.

She knew she was truly countrified, also perhaps rather stupid in resenting the fact that they were wasting their money.

When she reached her own bedroom, she had

not been there more than a few minutes before Mrs. Chambers came in.

"I thought you wouldn't stay up late, Miss Nola," she said, "so I waited up."

"That is very kind of you," Nola replied. "I expect you have spoilt the girls and let them go to bed early."

"Most of the ladies have their maids with them," Mrs. Chambers replied, "and there's no point in tiring out th' girls for nothing."

"I agree." Nola smiled.

She stepped out of her gown and Mrs. Chambers hung it up in the wardrobe.

"Now you get your beauty sleep, Miss Nola," she said, "and you'll be ready to enjoy yourself riding at seven o'clock, which is more than any of these painted and powdered ladies'll be doing."

There was a note of disapproval in her voice, which made Nola smile.

Then Mrs. Chambers said "Goodnight" and she was alone.

She went to the wardrobe to take down the cotton dress she had slipped into her trunk when Nanny was not looking.

It was very simple and might easily be taken for one of the gingham gowns the housemaids wore.

Then she went to the door and listened.

Everything was very quiet.

The party had not yet come upstairs.

If the ladies'-maids were awake, they were in their own rooms waiting for the bell.

Nola went to the linen cupboard.

Amongst the sheets, towels, and pillowcases there were the aprons that the housemaids wore and also their caps.

Hurriedly she took both and went back to her own room.

She only hoped there was no light by the side door which she had to open later.

If the Stranger—or Cousin Basil, whichever it was—thought she was Betsy, he would not make any comment.

But if he did, she would have to say she had taken Betsy's part at the last moment because Betsy was ill.

There was a chance that he would be suspicious.

Then he might go away without, as he intended, seeing the Earl in a compromising position, in which case there was nothing she could do about it.

Having gone so far, she could only hope that everything would go off in the way the Earl wanted.

She glanced at the clock on the mantlepiece.

There was still a long wait before the party came to bed.

Because Nola was afraid of falling asleep, she looked for a bookcase.

She found one which contained a few rather frivolous novels, a Bible, and an autobiography written by one of the Lings in the last century.

As that seemed the most appropriate to keep her awake, Nola took it from the case.

Having dressed herself in the gingham frock, she sat down on the sofa.

She was nearly asleep when half-an-hour later she heard the house-party coming up to bed.

They certainly were making no secret about it.

The men were laughing and obviously saying things to the women which made them give little shrieks of surprise or horror.

They passed Nola's door, moving along the corridor at the end of which was the Master Suite.

She could only hope that nothing had gone wrong with getting the *Contessa* out of the room next to the Earl.

Then she told herself she was quite certain that he would have done everything they planned punctiliously, in which case all that was left was for her to let the Stranger and the man with him in through the garden door and up the stairs.

It all seemed quite easy when she thought about it.

Yet, nearly half-an-hour later, as she walked towards the door, her heart was beating so wildly, she thought it might be heard.

She had put on the apron and the lace-trimmed cap which the housemaids wore.

When she looked out, she was relieved to find that the corridor was far darker than usual.

In the past every third sconce was kept alight.

The rest were extinguished by the footmen after the guests had gone to bed.

Tonight every fourth sconce had been left alight.

Although it was possible to see one's way, it would not be easy, Nola thought, to recognise a face.

She slipped down the staircase which was on the opposite side of the corridor to the Master Suite.

There was a thick carpet on the stairs which silenced her footsteps.

When she reached the passage at the bottom, she saw the door ahead of her which led out into the garden.

She was aware, because it had glass inserted into it, that that was where the light was coming from.

She went down the last stairs.

Even as she did so, she was aware there were shadows of two people standing outside.

Slowly, so as not to make a sound, Nola opened the door.

She kept well behind it as she did so, and was not surprised when a man pushed his way in.

He was followed by another, wearing a dark coat.

His collar was turned up and a soft cap pulled low over his forehead.

'That is how a detective should look,' Nola thought.

Then she was aware that the Stranger, whom she could not see very clearly, was waiting for her to go up first.

She moved quickly past him.

She averted her face as if she were looking for the bannister on which to put her hand.

As she walked up step by step, she was aware the men behind her were moving just as quietly as she was.

She reached the top of the staircase.

Now, in front of her, was the elaborate door leading into the Master Suite.

Beside it was the door into the next bedroom.

Nola drew in her breath.

The only thing that could go wrong now was if she had brought the Stranger up too soon and the Earl was not waiting for him.

They had come to a halt.

She was just about to move away, when the Stranger put out his hand and touched hers.

It was then she realised that he was giving her the twenty pounds he had promised Betsy.

She took it quickly.

She thought it was something she would return

to the Earl tomorrow, as in her opinion it was blood-money.

Then, with a backward look at the man behind him, Basil Ling stepped forward.

Crossing the corridor, he put his hand on the door next to that of the Master Suite.

Just for a moment he paused.

Although he had his back to her, Nola was sure he had an expression of triumph in his eyes.

He had won, he had got here!

He was putting his Cousin in a degrading position from which he could not escape.

With a gesture that was almost theatrical, he flung open the door.

Then, as the man in the dark coat followed him, Nola heard the Earl exclaim:

"Good Heavens, Basil! What on earth are you doing here at this time of night?"

chapter four

NOLA had a quick glance at the Earl, who was standing in front of the Dressing-Table.

He was wearing a robe which was undone and he was obviously just about to get into bed.

All the candles were lit in the room.

It was quite obvious that the bed was empty and there was no-one else there.

Nola moved quickly down the corridor.

Then, because she was curious as to Basil's reply, she could not help but stop halfway.

"What are you doing in this room?" Basil asked, as if he could not help but ask the question that was foremost in his mind.

Nola was sure that the Earl looked at him in surprise before he answered.

"I cannot see what that has to do with you. But, if you want to know, the late, lamented Earl had an extremely uncomfortable bed. I found it impossible to sleep last night and I can tell you the first thing I am going to buy for the house is a new mattress."

Nola thought this was a brilliant answer.

It prevented Betsy from being accused of giving Basil the wrong information.

Again there was a silence, and then the Earl

said in a good-humoured voice:

"Now, let me ask you again, what are you doing here, and who is your friend?"

"There has been a mistake," Basil muttered after a moment's pause.

Nola thought that perhaps he was turning round, ready to leave the bedroom.

She therefore moved very quickly the short distance to her own room.

She went inside and left the door ajar, and stood waiting to see what happened.

Now she could not hear what was being said.

She had the idea that the Earl was speaking somewhat sharply to his Cousin.

Then, through the crack in the door she saw Basil cross the corridor, followed by the detective.

He went down the stairs up which she had brought them.

She imagined they would go outside and shut the door behind them.

There was just a chance the Earl might come and thank her for what she had done.

He must be delighted at the way they had dealt with such a difficult problem, and now there could be no repercussions.

Then she heard the Earl shut the door of the bedroom he was in loudly, as if he wished to be overheard.

She supposed he was making it absolutely clear to Basil once and for all that that was where he intended to sleep, and alone.

She therefore shut her own door, undressed, and got into bed.

After all the excitement and waiting so long, she was tired and fell asleep.

Nola woke and realised that dawn had broken and she had slept all through the night.

She looked at the clock and saw it was just after six thirty.

She felt an irrepressible excitement because she could go riding.

She dressed herself very quickly and hurried down the stairs.

Already the housemaids were cleaning the fire-places.

There were two footmen in shirt-sleeves polishing the floor of the Hall.

She hurried down the front steps and walked quickly towards the stables.

She was wondering if the Earl would be there.

He came out of the stable door, followed by Groves, leading one of the outstanding horses.

It was, however, so restless that he found it hard to control.

"Oh, there you are!" the Earl exclaimed as Nola appeared. "I thought you would be too tired to go riding this morning."

Nola did not bother to reply.

She gave him a smile which told him better than words that nothing could be more important than riding.

Then she went to look for *Mercury*.

As no-one else appeared, she and the Earl set off a few minutes later, riding out of the stables into the paddock.

There was no need to ask where they were going.

Nola had showed him the flat ground yesterday.

She knew he was as eager as she was to set their horses galloping against each other.

They must have ridden for nearly a mile before they drew in their reins and the Earl said:

"That is better. Now I feel life is normal again. Thank you, Nola, for what you did last night."

She noticed that he addressed her by her Christian name, but merely said:

"You had . . . no more . . . trouble?"

"None at all," the Earl replied. "I imagine my Cousin has gone back to London with his tail between his legs."

"You cannot be sure," Nola said in a low voice. "He might try something else to get his own way."

It was difficult to put into words that his Cousin meant to kill him, but the Earl replied:

"Of course he will do that. He will never rest until he has got what he wants."

"How can you say it like that?" Nola said. "You will have to stop him. Is there no-one in your family who could talk to him and tell him to behave himself?"

"No-one that I know," the Earl said, "but then, as you are well aware, I was of no consequence until I came into the title."

"I am sure that is not true." Nola said, "but at the same time it makes things very difficult for you."

"I was thinking last night that it is almost an impossible situation," the Earl said, "so I might as well enjoy myself while I can."

"And you are enjoying yourself now," Nola said softly.

He bent forward to pat the neck of his horse.

"I have never had the chance to ride horses like this before. When I realised they were mine, I knew that above all things I wanted to go on living."

It was what Nola had wanted him to feel, and she felt a satisfaction within her heart.

Then she said:

"When Papa returns, you must talk to him. I am sure he will be clever enough to think of a way to handle your Cousin and perhaps . . . pay him . . . off.''

She said the last words rather tentatively in case it seemed impertinent.

"I have already thought of that," the Earl answered, "but I was told by a friend of mine that when he was boasting at the Club he would be rid of me and take my place here, someone said:

" 'Why do you not make your Cousin give you a large allowance so that it will be worthwhile keeping him alive?' "

"And what did your Cousin reply?" Nola asked.

"His reply was," the Earl said:

" 'Why should I be satisfied with a few slices when I can have the whole loaf?' "

Nola sighed.

"He is horrible," she said. "I feel he cannot be real."

"Unfortunately," the Earl replied, "he is very real. You should have seen the expression on his face when he had not caught me red-handed, as he expected. You realise he is almost insane in his desire to be rid of me?"

"Then what can we do?" Nola asked.

"That is what I am waiting for you to tell me," the Earl answered. "You saved me once, and now I regard you as my keeper. And quite frankly, Nola, I am afraid to be without you."

"We will think of something. I am sure we will think of something," Nola said reassuringly.

At the same time, she knew it was going to be very difficult.

She took the Earl the way she always went herself, over the flat land to a field where there were some excellent hedges to jump, and back through the woods which she loved.

She did not say anything, but she felt in a way

he understood how much the woods meant to her, that he was as thrilled as she was at the sunshine coming through the leaves and at the rabbits rustling in the undergrowth and the twisting, moss-covered paths they followed.

When finally they emerged into the Park, the Earl, who had not spoken for some time, said:

"Thank you, Nola, I enjoyed that. Now it is time for breakfast."

"And you will feel far more hungry," Nola said, "than you would if you had been in London."

"I am realising that without you preaching at me," the Earl replied. "I thought we would ride again after breakfast."

Nola shook her head.

"It is Sunday," she said, "and I must go to Church."

She looked at the Earl as she spoke.

After a few seconds he said:

"You are not suggesting it is traditional?"

"If the Head of the family is well enough," Nola answered, "he reads the Second Lesson."

The Earl did not speak, and after a moment Nola said:

"I am not preaching at you, but you do understand that after what the villagers have heard about your parties in London and not seeing you as soon as you arrived, it would be very exciting for them if you were in the family pew at eleven o'clock."

The Earl did not reply.

As they rode on, heading towards the lake, Nola wondered if she had made a mess of things.

She had been trying to think how she could suggest that the Earl should meet the people on the Estate.

She could not find the right moment to make this suggestion.

Now that he was silent, she glanced at him nervously until he said:

"If I agree to what you want, will you ride with me this afternoon and show me more of my Estate than I saw this morning?"

"And you will come to Church?" Nola cried. "Oh, that is marvellous! It is exactly what you should do, and I cannot tell you how thrilled everyone will be."

"I doubt if they will be as enthusiastic as you suggest," the Earl said somewhat sarcastically. "But I suppose it is one way I can thank you for last night."

"That reminds me," Nola said. "Your Cousin gave me the twenty pounds when they reached the bedroom door. I have it for you here."

She felt in the pocket of her riding habit as she spoke.

"Put it in the Offertory box," the Earl said hurriedly. "If it has come from my Cousin, I am quite sure it is tainted money and I would not deign to touch it."

"I will do what you say," Nola replied. "You really will come to Church at eleven o'clock?"

The Earl did not speak, and she went on:

"You must drive down in a carriage. The Vicar who is taking the Service in Papa's absence will meet you at the door and escort you to the family pew."

She thought the Earl was somewhat surprised, but she went on:

"When it is time to read the Lesson, you will find a Bible open on the Lectern and a piece of paper telling you how many verses to read."

She thought there was a faint and somewhat mocking smile at the corner of the Earl's mouth.

She went on quickly:

"The Vicar in this parish has always had strict instruction from the Earl not to preach for more than ten minutes, and when the Service is over he escorts you first to the porch, where your carriage will be waiting."

"I see you have everything arranged," the Earl said in a slightly mocking tone. "If I play the good little boy, what is my reward?"

"A very long ride in the afternoon," Nola replied, "so that you will be too tired when you get home to worry about anything, not even your Cousin Basil."

The Earl laughed, and it was a spontaneous sound.

"Very well," he said, "I agree, and I only hope you will not be disappointed at my performance."

"I have a feeling that despite the fact that you are mocking what I suggest," Nola said, "you will enjoy every moment of it."

Because she felt she had said too much and the Earl might change his mind, she urged *Mercury* forward.

He caught up with her only as they were entering the stables.

As she dismounted, he heard her say to Groves:

"Please can I have *Sunbeam*?"

"Of course, Miss Nola," Groves replied.

"Where are you going?" the Earl asked as the Groom disappeared into the stable.

"I am going home," Nola said, "to let everyone know that you are coming to Church. It is going to be the greatest excitement for the village since Guy Fawkes Night two years ago, when your predecessor gave us fireworks."

The Earl laughed, and it was again a very spontaneous sound.

"Now you are really making me want to run away. I suppose I must try and be a man and face the firing squad."

"On the contrary, it is a Royal progression, and you are King for a day."

The Earl laughed again.

As Nola rode home, she was wondering how she could make sure that everyone in the village could see their Landowner for the first time.

She had the answer as she rode out of the Lodge gates and saw the children all going to Sunday School.

She drew in her horse.

Most of them bade her politely, "good morning" as they had been taught to do.

"I have got good news," she said. "I want you to be clever enough to tell everyone in the village."

"What's that, Miss?" one of the elder girls asked.

"The Earl is coming to Church at eleven o'clock. I know you will all want to see him and so will everyone else. If you will hurry round and tell everyone in the village immediately after you have finished Sunday School, I will ask Nanny to have a gingerbread cake for each one of you at the Vicarage at tea-time this afternoon."

Nanny's gingerbread cakes were famous.

They were what the children enjoyed at Christmas and were also usually given by her Father on their Birthdays.

There was a hoot of joy, and they said:

"We'll tell everyone, Miss Nola."

"Do not leave anyone out," Nola said, "and of course you must be there yourselves."

Some of them often came to the Services with their Parents.

But her Father had not made it compulsory.

As they had Sunday School, he thought it a mistake for them to have too much Church.

"People are surprised to hear you say that, Papa," Nola had remarked.

"One can have too much, even of a good thing," her Father had said wisely. "I want the children to enjoy coming to Church and not to become bored because they are forced to do so."

As she rode on to the Vicarage, Nola hoped that she would not bore the Earl by making him do things he had no wish to do.

At the same time, it was important that his people, because he was their Landlord and their employer, should have the right idea about him.

He had a lot to live down, especially the stories Mrs. Kettle had been telling and what they had been hearing for the last year from London.

"It is not going to be easy," Nola told herself, "but they will be surprised and delighted to see him in Church today."

When she got home and told Nanny what had happened, Nanny said:

"Well, at any rate, that is a step in the right direction. I wondered last night if the dinner-party you were attending would be half as bad as Mrs. Kettle says it would be."

"There was nothing particularly wrong with it," Nola answered, "except if you ask me, the ladies were over-dressed and because they gambled at cards and Roulette, I suppose the village would think they were moving towards the fires of Hell."

"Gambling!" Nanny exclaimed. "For large sums or small ones?"

Nola thought of the ladies extorting money from the men to pay for their losses!

She knew perfectly well that her Mother would disapprove, and so would her Father.

She had no wish to tell a lie and therefore evaded an answer.

"I did not gamble! Anyway, I had no money to do so," she said, "and actually everyone went to bed quite early."

"Well, that sounds more sensible," Nanny said. "If you ask me, that Mrs. Kettle's capable of exaggerating a straight wall into a drunken one if it suited her."

Nola changed the subject.

When she had eaten her breakfast, she went upstairs to put on her best gown and the hat that went with it.

She could not help hoping that none of the ladies at the house-party would think it a good idea to accompany the Earl to Church.

That would certainly cause a sensation!

Their painted faces would astound the village and their hats and dresses would seem as outrageous as their evening gowns.

"If they come," she told herself, "even if it is only one of them, it will spoil the whole effect of the Earl meeting his people for the first time in Church."

It was exactly the sort of situation which her Father would have thought of and which in his own magical way he would make extremely successful.

Nola could only get to the Church early and pray that nothing would go wrong.

If the Earl changed his mind at the last moment, it would be a terrible anti-climax.

The Church was as old as the Hall.

A previous Earl had given it very attractive stained-glass windows.

The family pew of the Lings was carved with statues of Angels.

Nola remembered that her Mother, five years

77

ago, had re-covered the high Hassocks with red velvet.

She had also added comfortable red velvet cushions to the pews themselves.

There was, of course, the family pew in the Chancel.

When the Earl sat in it, he had a carved canopy over his head which looked very regal.

Nola had picked the flowers ready for the Church on Friday morning.

Because she wanted to go riding, Nanny had arranged them for her.

The sunshine was pouring through the windows and the flowers scented the air.

When Nola looked at the Church with its fine Memorials to the Ling family, she thought, no-one could help being impressed by it.

As the villagers filed in, Nola was listening all the time for the sound of the wheels on the drive.

The Vicar from the next village came down the Aisle in his Surplice and stood waiting at the porch door.

She felt then as if her heart would stop beating because she was so afraid something had gone wrong and the Earl would not turn up.

It was an immense relief when she saw the horses in the distance.

Just as she had planned, he was arriving two or three minutes before eleven o'clock.

The carriage drew up outside the Church and the footman got down from the box to open the door.

Nola felt like cheering because he was actually there.

As he stepped out, she realised that he had "done her proud" as Nanny might have said.

He was wearing a frock coat, a top hat, and

an orchid in his bottonhole.

The Vicar stepped forward, they shook hands, and he led the Earl into the Church.

Almost every pew was full, and there was also, Nola was aware, a number of children outside.

The organ was playing softly.

As the Earl came in through the West door, the congregation rose to its feet.

Although they had not been told to do so, it was a spontaneous welcome to a man who actually controlled their destiny.

The Earl took his rightful place in the family pew.

Nola, who was in the front seat of the congregation, thought he looked very impressive.

Her Father had arranged Matins so that it was a happy service and one in which the children could join in.

He always insisted on a large choir from the village.

Because he was extremely musical, they were surprisingly good.

As if today they were specially inspired, they sang with gusto.

They made the psalms seem more joyous than they had ever been before.

The Vicar preached a very simple sermon for exactly ten minutes.

After the blessing he waited to take the Earl back to the porch.

It was then, to Nola's surprise, he acted on his own initiative.

He went halfway down the Church and stopped to speak to some old men and women who were obviously pensioners.

He shook each one by the hand.

Then those in the pews in front and behind

theirs were eager to do the same.

In a minute or so everyone who attended the service wanted to meet the Earl personally.

Finally, without seeming to do so, he moved a little towards the porch.

He had in fact shaken hands with everyone.

He then thanked the Vicar for an excellent service and got back into his carriage.

Now the children and a number of the grown-ups cheered as he drove away.

He raised his top hat, and Nola was certain the smile on his lips was one of triumph.

"He enjoyed it, he really enjoyed it," she told herself.

Then she remembered how he said on several occasions how unimportant he had been before he became Earl.

She was quite certain that this was a new experience for him, one in which he would not be human if he did not find it enjoyable.

She had no idea that, as the Earl drove back alone towards the Hall, he was thinking how very different his life was to what it had been before.

This was also something different to what he had experienced in London.

He was actually thinking, and it would have pleased Nola to know it, that he must never again make the mistake of bringing his London friends to the country.

More important still, he had no intention of leaving the country until he had ridden every horse in his stables.

Nola went back to the Vicarage and changed into her riding habit.

If she was riding with the Earl in the afternoon as he had promised, there was no point in changing again for luncheon.

She thought she would look no more extraordinary in her plain but well-cut habit than the Earl's guests in their frills and furbelows and gowns far more suited to London than the country.

When she went into the room where they were meeting before luncheon, she saw that the Earl had already changed into riding clothes.

Actually the first words she heard someone say were:

"You are not going riding again this afternoon, are you, Rollo?"

"I have an appointment to keep," the Earl said as he saw Nola enter, and his eyes were twinkling.

"I thought at least," the *Contessa* said, "you would come and see me off at the Station."

Nola was instantly alert.

So the *Contessa* was leaving while the rest of the party were staying until Monday!

Nola had no idea that last night the Earl had gone to the new room in which the *Contessa* was sleeping.

This was after she had been told that the fire was smoking in her bedroom.

He waited until he was sure everyone was asleep, even if they had been woken by Basil and the detective moving about.

He had then gone into her room.

As he entered, the *Contessa* had sat up in her bed and said reproachfully:

"What has happened, why are you so late? I had almost fallen asleep."

"I did not dare come before," the Earl said, "but I am afraid I have very bad news for you."

He saw an apprehensive expression in the *Contessa*'s beautiful dark eyes.

When he told her that a detective sent by her

husband had actually come into the house, she gave a cry of terror.

"How could he dare do such a thing? What did you say to him? How could he know I am here?"

"I think you must face the fact," the Earl said quietly, "that your husband loves you and is also very jealous. I am surprised that he has not had you watched before."

"I could not imagine he would do such a thing," the *Contessa* said.

She had gone very pale, and the Earl was well aware how perturbed she was.

"Everything is all right," he said soothingly. "I sent the man away, convinced that he had caught me, unaware I was not, as he expected, with you. Although he has left the house, it is a great mistake for me to stay here with you for more than a few minutes. I am sure you will agree it would be best if you went back to London tomorrow."

"Of course I must do that," the *Contessa* replied. "But I still cannot believe that Pietro would behave in such an appalling manner."

The Earl gave a faint smile.

"Perhaps he has had reason to doubt your fidelity in the past," he said.

"Of course not," the *Contessa* said. "I have never, never been unfaithful to Pietro until, dear Rollo, I met you."

The Earl was quite certain this was a lie, but he was not prepared to argue about it.

Instead, he said:

"You know how deeply honoured I am that I should mean anything in your life, but we still have to think about your future."

The *Contessa* shivered and murmured:

"For all we know, the detective may be

watching this room now."

"I think that is unlikely," the Earl said. "But at the same time, we must take no chances."

"No, of course not," the *Contessa* agreed, "and, as I have already said, Rollo Darling, I will go back to London, but how, how, with Pietro feeling like this, will we ever see each other?"

"It will indeed be very difficult," the Earl said gravely, "and perhaps for some time, at any rate, we should be on our guard."

"I shall certainly be that," the *Contessa* said.

She put out her hand and gave a little sob.

"I love you, Rollo. You are the most handsome man I have ever met and a very wonderful lover. But I must protect my position in the social world, and most especially with the Royal Family in Italy."

"Of course you must," the Earl said. "Now, go to sleep and forget that all this disagreeableness has happened, and remember how much we enjoyed ourselves last night."

"It was wonderful, quite, quite wonderful," the *Contessa* said in a very different tone.

She put out her arms and pulled the Earl down towards her.

"You do . . . not . . . suppose," she whispered.

"No!" the Earl said firmly. "It is too dangerous. I have turned the man out of the house, but he may still be in the garden, seeking an opportunity of surprising us, as he intended to do."

The *Contessa* gave a little scream of horror and her arms were no longer tightly round the Earl's neck.

He kissed her gently and walked towards the door.

"You are very beautiful," he said. "Thank you for the happiness you have given me."

The *Contessa* gave a little sob.

When he was outside the door, the Earl thought again he had had a very lucky escape.

If Nola had not been brave enough to come and tell him what was happening, he knew exactly what sort of situation he would have been facing in the future.

He went back to his own room and turned the key in the door.

Before he went to sleep, he was thinking of Nola rather than the beauty of the *Contessa*.

When the Earl rose in the morning he made a resolution that he would never again take such risks.

He could understand all too well how the Italian felt.

How was he to keep his wife to himself?

Unless he could shut her up behind prison bars, there would always be men like himself overwhelmed by her beauty.

As Nola had discovered, every woman in the house party was married.

Because they were English and belonged to the *Beau Ton*, their husbands had two courses of action.

They could simply be indifferent to the way they behaved.

The alternative was to accept that their wives took an occasional lover, but with the deepest discretion.

If their wives' behaviour affected the honour of their name, they were bound to take her to the country.

They also quite naturally rebelled if they became a joke in the Clubs.

The husbands went hunting, shooting, or fishing and did not ask too many questions about what occurred when they were away.

It was quite obvious that foreigners like the *Conte* were not so complacent.

The Earl told himself for the thousandth time he had had an extremely lucky escape.

It would certainly be a mistake to push his luck too far.

He had therefore arranged for the *Contessa* to be seen off at the Station by Sir Richard Cross.

He had also suggested Lord Longdon should accompany her, but he refused.

"Do your own dirty work, Rollo," he said. "You know as well as I do that Edie will make a terrible scene if I appear in any way to be interested in the *Contessa*."

When luncheon was finished, the *Contessa* left first.

For one minute in the hall her fingers quivered in the Earl's as he raised them to his lips.

Then, as the women kissed her goodbye, she walked down to the open carriage which was to take her to the Station.

As the feathers fluttered on her hat in the wind and the diamonds glittered in the sunshine, she looked amazingly lovely.

'Yet,' Nola thought, 'rather like a Bird of Paradise in a chicken pen.'

As the horses drew away, the Earl gave a sigh of relief.

Then, as the horses were brought from the stables, he helped Nola into the saddle.

He had made arrangements to amuse his other guests.

Because the women did not wish to ride, they were to go driving and visit a Folly that Nola had told him about.

It was on top of one of the hills on the West side of the Estate.

"It has a fantastic view," Nola said, "and

there is a telescope through which you are supposed to see five counties."

It was, the Earl thought, as good an excuse as any other to keep the party amused and out of the way.

As he and Nola moved swiftly away from the house, she said:

"I feel rather as if we were playing truant. I am sure your men friends were eager to go on riding your horses."

"They cannot have their cake and eat it too," the Earl replied. "And as you well know, Nola, hell hath no fury like a woman scorned."

Nola laughed.

She knew as she did so that the Earl was concentrating on his riding and enjoying every minute of it.

Because he said he had never had a horse of his own, she had been afraid he was not a good rider.

But she admitted it would be impossible for anyone to be a Ling and not an equestrian.

She was aware in some ways that the Earl was not as skilled on a horse as William had been.

But at the same time he was a natural rider and that was what really counted.

They rode for a long way before the Earl asked:

"Where are you taking me?"

"To one of your best and most loyal farmers. He has had a tremendous struggle this last year to keep his head above water because he could not afford to drill the seeds the land needed or to buy new stock for the farm."

"I thought this would be another lesson," the Earl murmured.

"You might as well get them all over with," Nola said. "I have not yet told you how magnificent you were in Church. I was very proud of you."

"I thought you would be," the Earl said, "and though I was afraid I might make a fool of myself, it all seemed to come quite naturally to me."

"Of course it did, with the Ling blood in your veins," Nola said, "and all the village will now be talking of you with admiration instead of in shocked whispers."

"Is that what they have been doing up to now?" the Earl asked.

"But of course," Nola answered. "Your parties in London stunned them, to begin with."

The Earl stared.

"How could they know about my parties in London?" he asked.

"Very easily," Nola replied.

She explained how at least three people in the village had daughters in Ling House in Park Lane.

Also the children of other local inhabitants were working in London.

They sent home every bit of gossip there was about the Ling family.

When she finished speaking, the Earl exclaimed:

"Is there no privacy for someone like me!"

"Very little," Nola answered. "But then, one should not need privacy unless one is doing something wrong."

There was a little pause.

Then the Earl asked:

"Do you think I was doing wrong and were you shocked by my behaviour?"

"I would have been if Papa had not said that as a young man you had had no chance to sow your wild oats. You were therefore sowing them a little older than usual."

The Earl laughed.

"I never expected to meet someone like you, Nola," he said, "just as I never expected to be an Earl, to be rich, and to move in the social circles in London where women are as beautiful as the *Contessa* and yet behave in a very different way to what I expected."

"The truth is," Nola said quietly, "you stepped from your old world into a new one and everything is an excitement and an adventure. You would be inhuman if you did not enjoy the variety."

The Earl glanced at her.

"That is certainly wisdom," he said. "Thank you, Nola, for making it so clear."

He spurred his horse forward as he spoke.

She had the feeling he did not wish to talk about it any more.

They went on towards the farm, where the farmer was overcome with delight at meeting the Earl.

He told him all his problems, and Nola was glad that the Earl listened so intently.

He also promised to help in the most practical manner.

As they rode back towards the house, she said:

"You have made a lot of people happy today, and I know Papa will be very pleased when he comes home."

"Are you pleased?" the Earl asked.

"You know I am," Nola answered. "You have been completely marvellous and now, on behalf of the Estate, the village, and everyone else over whom you rule . . . thank you . . . very much indeed."

There was a little throb in her voice as she said "thank you" simply because she was so grateful.

It was so marvellous to feel that once again a

Ling was looking after his people and not failing them.

As she rode on, she thought it strange that while she had hated the Earl at first, he had now made her extremely happy.

chapter five

WHEN they were driving back to the house and had nearly reached the village, Nola said:

"When the rest of your guests leave tomorrow, I will have to go too."

"As it happens," the Earl said, "most of them are leaving about eleven o'clock, but Harry Longdon and Richard Cross want to stay on."

He gave a little smile before he added;

"They are finding my horses more attractive than women, and that is certainly something new."

Nola laughed, but she said a little uncomfortably:

"That will still . . . mean there is . . . no chaperon for me and . . . therefore I must . . . return to the . . . Vicarage."

"I have thought of that already." the Earl said, "and I was wondering if you know of anyone who would come and stay for a few nights. I have no wish to be alone even when Harry and Richard leave."

Nola felt her heart leap.

She had no wish to go back to the Vicarage with just Nanny to talk to.

She had no idea how long her Father would be before he returned.

Lord Longdon's friend Edie, who actually was Lady Edith Fairchild and the daughter of a Duke besides being married to a very distinguished Politician, had been very disagreeable.

"I want Harry with me in London," she said to the Earl. "I consider it very tiresome of him to be tempted into staying with your horses."

"I had no idea myself that I had such excellent stables," the Earl said, "and, like Harry, I am tempted to stay in the country forever."

Lady Edith gave a cry of protest.

"Horses, horses," she squealed, "do men ever think of anything else?"

"I am sure Harry thinks of you," the Earl said soothingly, "but these are exceptional animals, and you must allow him just a few days to enjoy them."

"Well, I personally am going back to London," Lady Edith said crossly, "and if I am not waiting for Harry when he returns, that is his fault."

The Earl said nothing, but it had crossed his mind that Nola could not stay without a chaperon.

Because she had saved him from the *Conte,* he thought of her as a mascot.

He had no wish to lose what he thought was her magic touch.

He was well aware of what would have happened by now if she had not been brave enough to save him.

He therefore said in a more earnest tone than he had used before:

"There must be someone whom we can ask."

"Yes, of course there is," Nola replied. "I am sure you will like her very much, and she is actually a relation of yours."

"Who is?" the Earl enquired.

"Lady Castleford," Nola said. "She was married to a distant Cousin of the Countess when she was very young and after they had been married for only five years he had a heart attack which killed him."

"So she is a widow," the Earl said. "How old?"

"I think she is only twenty-three," Nola said. "She is a very sweet and gentle person. She has a rather large and ugly house on the outskirts of the village."

She sighed before she went on:

"I often think how lonely she must be without a husband or any children. Her family live in the North, so she seldom sees them."

"I will write a letter as soon as we get home, asking her to come and stay," the Earl said, "and then Harry and Richard can leave when they want to and you will still be here to protect me."

"I hope that is what I can do," Nola said, "but it is rather a formidable task."

The Earl did not argue because he knew she was speaking the truth.

But he changed the subject as if even to think of his Cousin made him angry.

As it was the last night, the party seemed to drink more and be more noisy than they had been previously.

Nola watched the women flirting with the men who were their partners.

She found herself hoping that the Earl would not have many house-parties like this.

She was quite certain that the way everybody behaved, the noise they were making would all be repeated in the village.

Also one man knocked over several glasses and broke them.

She was so eager that the good impression the

Earl had made by going to Church would not be spoilt by tales about his friends.

To her relief, he insisted that they should go to bed before midnight.

As they went through the hall, he said to her in a voice no-one else could hear:

"Seven o'clock in the stables."

She smiled at him and then hurried to her own room.

She was in fact tired and slept as soon as she was in bed.

The Earl, however, lay awake, wondering if she heard, as he did, his friends moving about the corridor.

They were, he thought, quite unnecessarily noisy about it.

He told himself once again that he had made a mistake.

He would never ask these particular friends to Hallington Hall again.

"If I see them in London," he told himself, "that is one thing, but they are out-of-place here and I suspect my ancestors are frowning at me, although Nola maybe is the only person who is aware of it."

He was thinking of how much more there was to see on his Estate, also how many farmers and employees there were to meet.

Then finally he fell asleep.

As he had expected, none of his men friends wished to join him in riding before breakfast.

He had heard Harry and Richard saying last night that they would ride as soon as they had seen their lady friends into the train.

He thought it very unlikely they would feel strong enough to join him and Nola at an early hour.

He was correct in this.

When he arrived at the stables he found Nola already making a fuss of *Mercury*, who had been brought from his stall into the yard.

He thought as she smiled at him how fresh she looked.

It was a relief to see a woman without a painted and powered face.

The Earl was soon mounted on a horse he had not ridden before.

Then they set off on their usual route towards the flat land.

There was no doubt that the new horse which the Earl was riding was extremely swift and also hard to hold.

After they had galloped, they sailed over the hedges in style.

Nola noticed that the Earl's new mount was an even better jumper than the one he had ridden the day before.

"I think we shall have to find some higher hedges," she said when they finished.

"I was thinking that I might build jumps in one of the paddocks," he said, "and then we will know exactly how high each of my horses can jump."

Nola gave a cry of delight.

"That would be very exciting! It would also be very interesting to know exactly what was the top height of every horse you owned."

"That is what I shall do," the Earl said.

He talked about it enthusiastically as they rode beside a stream.

Nola told him there were some small trout in it, and she used to fish there when she was a child.

"Are there any fish in the lake?" the Earl asked.

"Of course there are," Nola answered. "Papa very much enjoys catching quite large trout. He always insists that we put back the small ones."

"I will have to talk to your Father about that and many other things," the Earl said.

They turned into the woods.

Once again Nola was entranced by their beauty.

Today the sunshine was very bright.

Although the leaves were getting thicker, it still shone on the mossy path and turned it to gold.

"I know this is your special place," the Earl remarked.

"Wherever I go I always seem to end up here," Nola said.

"And you feel it is enchanted."

She looked at him in surprise.

"How do . . . you know . . . that?"

"I saw in your eyes what you were feeling the first time you brought me here," he said. "Now I understand and I am aware I am privileged to own anything so exciting."

"That is exactly what I want you to feel," Nola said. "And who could be more lucky than you to own such a magnificent Estate and such a wonderful house."

"I have been counting my blessings," the Earl said. "And that reminds me—I was going to ask you . . ."

As he spoke, they were both aware there was a sound of a horse behind them.

Nola turned her head in surprise, and so did the Earl.

Coming towards them on one of the horses from the stables was a young man.

He had been in the house-party, but Nola had hardly had a word with him.

His name was Eric Webstead.

He had been attached to a very exotic red-haired woman who appeared to be very possessive.

She had, in fact, though he seemed to enjoy it, monopolised him completely.

It was doubtful if he had a chance of speaking to anyone else.

Now, as he drew up beside them, he said to the Earl:

"I just missed you, but your groom told me which way you had gone, so now I have caught up with you."

"I am sorry, Eric," the Earl said, "but I had no idea you wanted to ride with us, or I would have suggested it."

"I was a fool not to suggest it myself," Eric Webstead replied. "Then this morning, when it was my last chance, I knew it was something I could not miss."

"Have you enjoyed the ride?" Nola asked softly.

"I took all the hedges in style," Eric said boastfully. "I wish you had seen me! I can hardly show off in a wood, can I?"

Nola gave a little laugh.

As she did so, there was suddenly a loud explosion.

It seemed to shriek through the air just beside them.

All the horses reared.

Nola was not quite certain what it was, but she had the greatest difficulty in holding in *Mercury*, while the Earl needed all his strength to prevent his horse from bolting.

The horse that Eric Webstead was riding tore ahead down the path, and there appeared to be no stopping him.

Then, just as Nola had pulled in *Mercury*, they heard Eric give a shout ahead of them.

At the same time, he seemed to stand up in the stirrups and reach with both hands over his head.

Both Nola and the Earl were staring at him in astonishment.

They realised he was swinging from the branch of a tree while his horse had gone ahead of him.

Swiftly, without speaking to each other, they rode towards him.

Just as they reached Eric Webstead, he dropped down on to the ground.

It was then Nola saw ahead that his horse had fallen.

As she drew nearer still, she could see the animal was fighting to get back onto his feet.

He had fallen into a narrow but deep ditch which had unexpectedly appeared in the ride.

It had never been there before and, as Nola stared at it, the Earl said:

"What happened, Eric? How did you manage to save yourself in such an extraordinary way?"

"I thank God it was something I learned when I was in the Cavalry," Eric Webstead replied. "Otherwise I would have fallen forward and very likely broken my neck."

It was then Nola gave a quick glance at the Earl.

Their eyes met and they knew they were both thinking the same thing.

Basil had done this.

Basil had known they would ride home this way and had hoped to kill he Earl.

Because Nola could see that the horse was injured, she held out *Mercury*'s rein to the Earl.

He took it without saying anything.

She jumped down and hurried to where Eric was now trying to pull his horse onto its feet.

The ditch had been very skilfully made.

It was difficult to notice until one had almost reached it.

Then Nola saw it was deep enough to catch a

horse's front legs and bring it crashing to the ground.

Eric Webstead's horse was trembling.

As he and Nola managed to pull it onto its feet, she saw that its front knees were injured and one was bleeding.

She patted the horse and made a great fuss of it.

Fortunately she had in her pocket three lumps of sugar.

She took these in her pocket to give to *Mercury* when they got back to the stables.

She patted and soothed Eric's horse, which she now remembered was called *Bluebird*.

She also gave him the lumps of sugar one by one, and he seemed a little less shaky.

"I will walk him home," Eric said, "but I cannot imagine, Rollo, why you have a ditch like this in your woods, because it is extremely dangerous."

"I am aware of that," the Earl replied, "and I can assure you it was not here yesterday when we came this way."

"Then who the hell has dared to do such a thing?" Eric asked.

Nola thought it would be a grave mistake for Mr. Webstead to know the truth.

She gave the Earl a warning glance, then realised he had thought the same as she had, because he replied:

"I can only imagine it was poachers. It seems early in the year, but of course it may be boys after rabbits who have no idea what they are doing."

"I should certainly have it filled in," Eric said.

"I thought it was so very clever of you," Nola said," to avoid the fall yourself. I have never seen anyone catch on the branch of a tree as you did."

"I told you it was something I learned when I

was in the Cavalry," Eric replied. "As I have not practised it for some years, I am only thankful that I managed to avoid being injured one way or another."

Nola thought he had been right when he said that if he had been thrown from *Bluebird*, he might easily have broken his neck.

She knew that was exactly what Basil had intended should happen to the Earl.

He was thinking the same.

They all walked back to the stables, Eric leading *Bluebird*.

Nola was thinking it was impossible to go on like this, not knowing from day to day what Basil would do next.

When the reached the stables, Groves was extremely upset at seeing *Bluebird*'s knees and that he was limping badly.

The Earl, however, managed to evade too many questions about what had happened in the woods.

When he and Nola walked to the house, leaving Eric still talking to Groves, he said:

"How could I have imagined he would think of anything like that?"

"Do you think he dug it himself? He must be very strong," Nola said.

"Oh, he is," the Earl replied. "When we were children he could always knock me down, and at school he terrified the younger boys."

Nola was thinking he must be exceedingly strong if he had dug anything so quickly.

"I am not exaggerating," the Earl said, "he has been extremely athletic all his life. He prides himself on being able to climb the highest mountain we have in this country and has, I believe, been one of the first men to climb Mont Blanc."

"Then what can we do about it?" Nola asked.

"That is the question I am asking myself," the Earl replied. "But I suppose sooner or later he will win."

They had almost reached the front steps by this time, and Nola stopped.

"You must not say that," she said. "It is unlucky! Of course he must not win. He is evil and evil will always lose in the end."

"I only hope you are right," the Earl said, "but I cannot be watched over for every twenty-four hours of the day and night. Heaven knows what he will try another time."

"We will just have to pray that we shall be cleverer than he is," Nola said quietly.

The Earl looked at her and smiled.

"Thank you, Nola," he said. "As I have told you already, I look on you as my mascot and I know you will not fail me."

"You will have to thank Mr. Webstead for saving you this morning," Nola said.

"It certainly seems a miracle that no-one was hurt except poor *Bluebird*," the Earl said.

"I will ride him as soon as he is better, to bring back his confidence," Nola promised.

Then she felt that perhaps she was being presumptuous.

The Earl might think she was taking for granted that she would always ride his horses.

He must have read her thoughts, because he said:

"Of course you must, and although I think you would rather protect the horses than me, we both need you."

"Then you have certainly given me a Herculean task," Nola said.

She was trying to speak lightly.

Then, as she went upstairs to her bedroom before going into breakfast, she thought that it had really been a terrifying experience.

How could that ghastly Cousin of the Earl's think of anything so wicked as to place what was actually a booby-trap on the ride they always took on their way home?

She was trying to think of how many other places on the Estate might be dangerous, but her head whirled!

It was impossible to be on their guard against everything they did and everywhere they went.

"It is getting more and more frightening!" she said aloud, and felt herself shiver.

She went down to breakfast and found the Earl and Eric inevitably discussing what had just occurred.

There was no-one else there.

"I think," Nola said quietly as she joined them at the Dining-Room table, "it would be a mistake to tell the others before they left, what had happened."

"Yes, of course," the Earl said quickly. "It would be exaggerated into a drama, and I have no wish for anyone in London to think my Estate is badly run."

"I will say nothing," Eric answered, "but you are lucky, Rollo, you do not have to explain to my family why I have a broken neck. And I am sure that Sylvia would be very annoyed."

As Sylvia was the red-headed beauty with whom he had been absorbed ever since he had come to the Hall, Nola thought this was an understatement.

However, she said nothing.

A few minutes later the door opened and Lord Longdon and Richard Cross came in.

Although they were going to the Station to say goodbye to their ladies, they were dressed in riding clothes.

It was obvious how they intended to spend the rest of the day.

When they saw the Earl and Nola in the Dining-Room, Harry said:

"I might have guessed you two would have been riding before it was light, but I did not expect to see Eric here."

"I have not had a chance to ride until now," Eric replied. "I am making it clear to Rollo that I am expecting another invitation very shortly and this time it had better be a 'men only' party."

They all laughed at this, and the Earl said:

"I think perhaps you would find it rather dull in the evenings, unless, of course, we had a Steeplechase every day and perhaps a midnight Point-to-Point with the rider allowed to use only one hand."

"Now you are thinking of what they did in the Regency," Nola said. "I have always believed it was very cruel to the horses."

"We will think of something unusual when the occasion arises," Harry remarked. "But I intend to ride your fastest and best horse this afternoon, Rollo, so I hope you do not want it yourself."

"There are plenty to choose from," the Earl answered. "Nola has had the good idea of having special jumps made so that next time you come you will be able to know exactly how high you have jumped without falling off."

"That is an insult, but I like the idea," Harry said. "The sooner you get on with it, the better."

Then they all began to discuss whether or not the Earl should build a race-course on his Estate.

Nola could see that he was intrigued by the idea and was considering it quite seriously.

'I am sure after this he will stay in the country,' she thought. 'Yet was the country even more dangerous than the town?'

She was terrified at the thought of how easily the Earl might have gone ahead and fallen into the trap which Basil has set for him.

It was only by the skin of his teeth and his training in the Cavalry that Eric had managed to escape.

As a foot soldier, the Earl had not had such opportunities.

'It would be too ignominious,' she thought 'if, having escaped from the *Mahdi*'s followers with only a wound, he was killed by his Cousin.'

Just one man against one man.

At the same time, what could they do?

She looked at the Earl sitting at the head of the table, laughing and talking with his friends.

It would be very cruel if, having just come into the title, the Estate and, of course, a fortune, he had to die through the sheer greed of a relative.

There was no doubt that Basil was utterly and completely despicable.

"Save the Earl, God, please save him," she prayed.

It was a very sincere prayer, and it came from the heart.

At the Earl's suggestion, Nola went off after luncheon to see Lady Castleford and ask her to come and stay at the Hall.

"It seems a strange request," he said, "but I feel if you will explain, she will understand, and, as you say, she is a relation."

"I expect she will be as excited as anyone else in the County at being asked to be your guest," Nola replied.

And of course she was right!

Nola found Lady Castleford in the garden of her house.

With the sunshine on her hair, she looked, Nola

thought, very pretty as she walked across the lawn towards her.

"I am surprised to see you, Nola," she said. "I heard that your Father was away and thought that perhaps you had gone with him."

"No, Papa has gone to his brother, who may be dead by now," Nola replied. "I stayed behind to look after the village and, of course, the new Earl who has just arrived at Hallington Hall."

"Oh, do tell me what he is like!" Gwen Castleford exclaimed.

"He is charming," Nola replied, "but rather bewildered at inheriting so much when he has always been so poor."

Gwen Castleford laughed.

"That sounds like a story from a novel. Is he good-looking like all the Lings?"

"He is very handsome and eager for you to come and meet him."

Gwen Castleford's eyes opened wide.

"I have come here," Nola said quickly, "to ask you if you would be very kind and chaperon me."

She explained there had been a large party.

Now some of the men wanted to stay on and she wanted to ride with them.

"I quite understand," Gwen Castleford said. "Of course, Dearest, if you want me, I shall be only too delighted to come to the Hall."

She gave a little sigh as she said:

"I often feel very lonely and, although my relatives come and stay with me from time to time, most of them are married and have children, so it is difficult for them to leave their homes."

Nola knew that Gwen was wishing that she had a child of her own, and she said:

"Here is your chance to meet some charming young men whom you ought to have met while you were a *débutante*."

Gwen Castleford laughed again.

"Do you know I went to only two Balls when I came out! Then I met Bernard and was married almost before I realised what was happening."

"You have got a lot to make up for," Nola said, "so hurry and pack your clothes and do not forget your riding habit. I am afraid they will talk 'horses, horses,' all the time."

"And I shall be quite prepared to listen to anything they condescend to say to me." Gwen laughed once more.

Nola went upstairs to help her pack.

There was a rather severe and somewhat disagreeable maid who produced the trunks.

When they were alone, she said:

"Surely you have some young servants? All the ones I have seen so far seem to be over fifty."

"They are," Gwen agreed. "They were with Bernard before I married him and they treat me rather as if I were an obstreperous child who has got into the house by mistake."

She was laughing as she spoke.

But Nola knew she was telling the truth and felt very sorry for her.

She made her put on one of her prettiest gowns and most becoming hat.

Then they drove back in the comfortable Chaise in which Nola had arrived.

"It was sweet of you to come and fetch me," Gwen said as they went towards the Hall. "I know you would much rather have been riding with the new Earl, and I feel guilty at taking you away from him."

"I have ridden this morning," Nola said, "and of course I wanted to come and explain to you why you were wanted without much ceremony to stay. I am very grateful to you for saying 'yes.'"

"I never imagined when I woke up this morning that anything so exciting was waiting for me," Gwen said, "but I must say I am very relieved that you are the only female there."

She paused as if she were looking back into the past, then went on:

"I am frightened of those London women who used to pursue Bernard and always talked to him as if I were not there."

Nola laughed.

"They have all left, I am glad to say, and in my opinion, although I was too polite to say so, they were over-dressed, over-painted, and they laughed too much."

"I know exactly what you mean," Gwen said. "They always made me feel small and insignificant, rather like a daisy among a lot of orchids."

"I felt the same," Nola said, "except that thankfully none of them wanted to ride and I gathered they were all 'Hyde Park trotters.'"

"I can still ride as well as I did when my Father first taught me," Gwen said, "but I have only two horses in the stables and I suppose it is rather stupid of me not to have bought more."

Nola was thinking it was sad that she had no-one to ride with.

She hoped that Harry and Richard would be nice to her and perhaps flirt with her a little.

They had certainly flirted with the ladies who had left them to return to London.

Gwen had, of course, been to the Hall before, when the last Earl was alive.

As they were going up the drive, she said:

"I had forgotten how big it is! What it wants is a large number of children to enjoy it and, of course, play hide-and-seek in the corridors."

"I have often thought that myself," Nola said.

She wondered if the Earl would marry, and felt

her heart sink at the thought.

If he did, it might be someone like the *Contessa*.

She would certainly not encourage visits from the Vicar's daughter.

Instead, she wold give large parties for London friends who would think country women like herself and Gwen too boring to be invited.

Yet, Nola thought, if the *Contessa* was the sort of woman the Earl deserved as a wife, he would find it difficult to find her.

Amongst the country families near them, most of the girls were sturdy and rather heavy.

Although they rode, they would not be able to keep up with the Earl.

Their conversation was certainly very different to that of the *Contessa* and her friends who had been at the Hall this weekend.

'I am sure there is no-one local who would interest him,' Nola thought.

Then she felt that when the excitement of the horses wore off, he would want to go back to London.

Then he would find a woman like the *Contessa*.

"You are looking sad, Nola," Gwen said unexpectedly. "You are not regretting you have asked me to come and stay with you?"

"No, of course not," Nola said, "it is very exciting to have you. I am just hoping that you will like the Earl and he will like you."

She need not have worried.

Although Gwen was now living by herself in the country, she had, when she first married, entertained a number of distinguished people. She had therefore learned not to be shy.

She was completely at ease with the Earl and with Harry and Richard.

Because she looked very pretty when they came in for tea, they paid her compliments.

Sooner than Nola could hope for, everyone was laughing at something Harry had said and the way he was pulling the Earl's leg.

There were only the five of them for dinner.

Yet Nola thought it was the most amusing party since she had first come to the Hall on Friday night.

They all seemed to be making jokes.

There was no question of anyone wanting to play cards after dinner.

They sat in comfortable armchairs and talked on many different subjects, and surprisingly hardly mentioned horses.

It was Gwen who said:

"I think we ought to go to bed although it is not yet midnight. If we are riding early in the morning, as Nola tells me we are, then we all need our beauty sleep."

"You have no need for yours, as you well know," Harry said.

Gwen did not blush, she merely replied:

"That is a very nice thing for you to say, I only hope it is true."

"I will have to prove it to you," Harry replied.

Gwen smiled at him.

It was so different to the flirting which had taken place last night and the night before, Nola realised, when every word spoken by the women from London seemed to have a different meaning.

They flashed their eyelashes which she rather suspected were mascaraed.

They pouted their lips and, at the same time, moved a little nearer to the man to whom they were talking.

"Nola and I are going to bed," Gwen said, "and I suggest you do not drink any more unless you wish us to prove tomorrow that we can both ride very much better than you."

Before anyone could reply, she put out her hand to the Earl.

"Thank you very much for having me to stay. It is very exciting for me to be here," she said. "I know at the moment it is exciting for you. Who could feel anything else in this wonderful house?"

The Earl kissed her hand and thanked her for coming.

Then he said to Nola:

"Seven o'clock. Do not be late, or we shall leave without you."

He was only teasing her, but Nola replied almost indignantly:

"You know I am never late."

Then her eyes met his.

Somehow they were saying something which could not be put into words.

She was not certain what it was.

Yet she felt a strange feeling in her breast that had not been there before.

It was as if they were both caught by a magic spell.

Then Harry cracked a joke and everyone was laughing.

Although she did not know what he had said, Nola laughed too.

Then, as she went upstairs with Gwen, she told herself that Rollo had really been warning her once again that she had to protect him from Basil.

'I am sure that is what he was trying to say,' she thought.

At the same time, she was not certain.

chapter six

By luncheon time the following day, Nola thought she had never been so happy or had such an amusing time.

They had ridden first thing, at seven o'clock, raced each other over the flat land, and cleared every jump.

The only difference to other days was that the Earl refused to come back through the woods.

"I have given orders for the ditch to be filled in," he said to Nola," but I think it is a mistake for us to go there for the moment."

Nola wondered whether he was thinking it had upset her because such a thing had happened in her beloved woods.

Alternatively, Basil might still be lurking in the undergrowth.

There was no explanation of how the explosion had gone off.

Because the Earl did not want his staff to talk about it, he had said nothing.

Only when he was alone with Nola did he say:

"I think it must have been automatic in some way, or Basil was there, hoping to pick me up in pieces."

"You must be careful, very, very careful," Nola said.

"I am relying entirely on you," he replied, which made her more nervous for him than ever.

They were finishing luncheon, and the servants had withdrawn, when Gwen said to the Earl:

"I have news for you which I think you will find awe-inspiring."

"What is it?" he asked.

"The maid who waits on me here has a sister who is employed by the Marchioness of Darnleigh."

She saw the Earl was listening but did not appear to be particularly interested, and she asked:

"You know who that is, of course?"

"I have no idea," he replied.

"The Marchioness was the sister of the late Earl. She was very important and all the Ling family are terrified of her."

"Why?" the Earl enquired.

"Because she made herself, when her brother was ill, the sort of materfamilias of the family."

"What you are saying," the Earl replied, "is that she interferes with the Lings and makes them do what she tells them."

"That is exactly right," Gwen agreed.

"But why should it be bad news for me?" the Earl enquired.

"Because once she knows that you are here at Hallington Hall, she will swoop down and, like most of the family, you will feel like a small boy at a preparatory school who has been sent for by the Headmaster."

Harry laughed at this.

"I know exactly what you mean," he said, "and Rollo had better look out or he will find himself stood in the corner for not behaving as a belted Earl should."

"Worse than that," Gwen said, "I know that she is determined to marry you off as soon as possible to what she considers a young woman suitable to be the Countess of Hallington."

"Then she will be disappointed," the Earl said sharply.

"You will find it very difficult to sidetrack her from anything she wants to do," Gwen warned.

She said it in such a way that the Earl replied:

"Surely you are not being serious."

"I am," she said. "You have no idea how the Marchioness bullies every member of your family with whom she comes in contact. Quite frankly, I am terrified of her."

"You will have to look out, Rollo," Richard said, "or you will find yourself going up the aisle with some blue-blooded young woman who cannot tell the difference between a horse and a donkey."

"That is just what might happen," Gwen said, "and I did hear when you first inherited that the Marchioness was very disappointed that there was not a more important member of the family to receive the title!"

She looked at him to see if he was angered at what she had said.

Then she went on:

"She said to one of the Lings, 'The first thing we must do is to see that he marries someone suitable to bear our very distinguished name.' "

"Well, I suppose I can be thankful," the Earl said, "that so far I have never met her. Perhaps if she wants to come and stay here, I can say the house is full or hide in the cellars."

"No-one yet has been able to avoid the Marchioness when she is on the warpath," Gwen warned. "But we will all come to your wedding and wish you luck."

She was teasing the Earl, but he said quite seriously:

"Whatever you may say, I am damned if I will marry anyone I do not want to. Forgive my language, but I feel very strongly on the subject."

"Of course you do," Gwen agreed. "At the same time, I must warn you that the Marchioness is very powerful in her own way. As a traditional Lady of the Bed Chamber and a close friend of Queen Victoria's, she sometimes asks Her Majesty's help when someone is reluctant to do as he is told."

"In which case," Harry said, "it becomes a Royal Command and there is no escaping."

"Now you are both frightening me," the Earl said, "and if you say any more, I shall leave immediately for Southern Asia or the North Pole!"

They all laughed.

Later, thinking it over, Nola could understand the Earl had been of no importance in the family until he inherited.

Now the older members, like the Marchioness, were bound to think it would be suitable if he married into one of the great and ancient English families.

The Lings went back to Richard Coeur de Lion, and members of the family had been distinguished Statesmen all down the centuries.

Somehow in her plans for the Earl wanting to build up his Estate, she had not thought of him marrying anyone.

There was obviously no chance of him marrying the *Contessa* nor any of the other ladies who had been staying at the Hall.

She thought of him only pursuing them in London.

But now he might come back with a bride who

would doubtless insist on everything being very different to what it was!

Then she told herself the Earl's marriage was not her business.

It would definitely be a great mistake for her to try to interfere.

Yet somehow what Gwen had said half jokingly at luncheon was like a dark cloud.

It depressed her all the afternoon.

The men had said that as a change from riding, they would try and catch some fish in the lake.

Nola was not surprised to find that both Harry and Richard were good fishermen and went to Scotland every autumn.

They both told her how many salmon they had caught the previous Season.

Harry was very proud of having caught one which weighed twenty pounds.

The Earl had obviously never fished a salmon river.

But because he was naturally athletic and had done a little fishing when he was a boy, he managed to everyone's surprise to catch the first fish in the lake.

It was only a two-pound trout, but he was delighted with it.

It made both Harry and Richard determined to beat him as quickly as possible.

It was all very amusing.

They laughed a lot, especially when Harry nearly fell in and got his legs wet.

Nola, however, kept thinking that if the Earl married some very grand young woman, it was doubtful if she would be welcome at the Hall.

There was no doubt in her mind that when the Marchioness arrived, she would not encourage the Earl to have a friendship with the Vicar's daughter.

"I like being here with him," she told herself rather piteously.

Then it suddenly occurred to her that what she felt for the Earl was different to what she had felt for any man before.

Granted there had been no young men in her life, so she had not really thought about love.

Now she watched the Earl.

He was so handsome, she told herself despairingly that she was falling in love.

"How could I be . . . so stupid . . . so insane?" she questioned. "There is every likelihood," she told herself sternly, "that when he has ridden all the horses, he will go back to London and never think of me again."

It hurt almost unbearably to think of that happening.

She therefore tried to talk to Richard and not watch the Earl.

Gwen was standing on the other side of the lake with Harry.

He was determined to catch a larger trout than anyone else.

So far he had succeeded in catching only such a small one that Nola had insisted on him throwing it back.

Now he was making Gwen laugh, and they were obviously both enjoying themselves.

The Earl was moving upstream alone.

Although Nola was trying to concentrate on Richard, she found her eyes following the Earl.

He got a bite, and as his rod bent, she found it impossible not to run up the bank towards him.

"You have caught a trout!" she exclaimed. "How big is he?"

"Enormous," the Earl replied.

"I do not believe it," Nola laughed. "Bring it in and I will land it for you."

She picked up the landing net and went down to the edge of the water.

The Earl climbed a little higher up the bank.

She netted the trout and it was about two pounds.

"It is not fair," Harry shouted across the lake, "I am casting far better than you, Rollo, and so far I have not had a bite."

"I think your talents lie in a different direction," the Earl replied meaningfully.

When ten minutes later Harry did catch a trout, he was delighted.

He swore it was three pounds at least.

Nola, however, thought it was not very much larger than the Earl's.

"I suppose," the Earl said unexpectedly, "I should have asked you if you wanted to fish. I am sure it is something you do very well."

"I would much rather watch you," Nola said.

"That is what I hope you are doing all the time," he said. "I find myself wondering where Basil will strike next."

"Do not think about him," Nola said quickly. "You have been lucky so far, and I feel your Guardian Angel is working overtime."

"I have a Guardian Angel," the Earl replied, "and she is a very pretty girl called Nola."

"Seriously," Nola said in a low voice, "I think you should get someone from the family to speak to Basil and tell him to behave himself. What about the Marchioness Gwen was telling us about?"

"I am sure she will be far too busy finding me a suitable wife," the Earl answered.

Nola did not answer, and after a moment he went on:

"I suppose you realise that when I have a son and heir, Basil will have to give up his murderous intentions? He could hardly kill two members of the family and still manage to avoid the gallows."

"I believe anything of a man who would dig that horrible trap in the woods," Nola said. "I think perhaps he is insane and what you should really do is to try to get him certified."

"On what evidence?" the Earl asked.

Nola made a little helpless gesture.

"That is the difficulty," she murmured. "We have nothing to prove what he intended to do to you as long as you are still alive."

As she spoke, she felt as if a knife were being thrust into her heart.

She could no longer pretend even to herself she did not love the Earl and wanted him to live.

How could he possibly die at the hand of his envious Cousin, when he was so handsome?

Also, so very different from what she had first thought him to be.

"I love him, I love him," she told herself.

She felt as if the birds overheard were repeating the words as they flew into the oak trees.

When all three men had caught several fish each, they went back in triumph to the house.

There was tea waiting for them in the Drawing-Room and a profusion of delicious things to eat.

There were hot scones, cucumber sandwiches, currant and iced cakes.

There was besides this a variety of small delicacies for which Mrs. Newman was famous.

Every child who had ever come to the Hall had been thrilled by them.

"If I stay here much longer, I shall get fat," Harry said.

"It is worth it to be in such a beautiful place," Gwen answered.

"And with two such beautiful women," Harry added.

He had included Nola, but she knew he was looking at Gwen.

He was flirting with her just as she had hoped he would.

'Surely he can see how much sweeter and nicer she is than the women who came down from London,' she thought.

What pleased her was that Gwen was looking very happy.

Although she laughed at Harry's compliments and made no attempt to reciprocate, she was obviously enjoying herself.

She looked even prettier than she had when she first arrived.

They went riding again for an hour after tea.

They came back to the Hall, having enjoyed the exercise, besides, as Richard said, all having an appetite for what undoubtedly would be a large dinner.

Nola and Gwen ran up the stairs together.

"I am enjoying every minute of being here," Gwen said. "Thank you for thinking of me. Rollo told me that it was entirely your idea that I should come here as your chaperon."

"I could not have thought of a better one," Nola said, "and you do see that the Earl is quite different to what we thought he was when we had just heard about his parties in London."

"I suppose when the excitement of being at the Hall wears off," Gwen said, "he will go back to Ling House in Park Lane."

She spoke quite casually.

Once again Nola felt that pain go through her.

She knew that when the Earl went back to London her heart would go with him.

Because she wanted to look her best, she put on her Mother's gown, the one she had worn the first night she arrived.

She knew it was more becoming than anything she owned herself.

When she went into the Drawing-Room she was almost sure there was an expression of admiration in the Earl's eyes.

Newman had made the dinner table small, as there were only five of them.

There was only one candelbrum in the centre of the table which threw a very becoming glow on the two young women.

Once again they were laughing quite spontaneously at Harry's jokes.

At the same time, he and Richard never stopped complimenting the two women who were with them.

They drank their health several times.

When dinner was over, Harry made it very clear he wanted Gwen to show him a certain picture they had been talking about which was in the Gallery.

They went off together.

When they had gone, Richard also made an excuse to leave the Earl and Nola alone.

"You look as if you are enjoying yourself," the Earl said unexpectedly.

"Of course I am," Nola replied. "Everyone was so witty at dinner, and I know that Gwen is happy. She is often so lonely all by herself."

"She must come to London and stay at Ling House," the Earl remarked.

It was the last thing that Nola expected him to say.

Then, as she thought he was planning to leave the country very soon, she wanted to cry out at the agony of it.

Because for a moment she felt as if her brain was not working very quickly, she murmured.

"Perhaps . . . it will . . . be more . . . dangerous

for . . . you in . . . London."

"I do not think it matters where I am," the Earl replied. "After what happened in the woods, I have actually been thinking how easy it would be for him to shoot me when I am next riding through it."

Nola gave a cry of horror.

"I cannot . . . imagine he . . . would do . . . that."

"Why not?" the Earl asked. "If he shot me dead and there were no witnesses, why should anyone imagine it was Basil if he was clever enough not to be seen in the neighbourhood?"

"So you would . . . rather go . . . back to . . . London?" Nola said.

The words seemed to come with difficulty through her lips.

"I am thinking about it," the Earl said.

When he had finished speaking, he coughed.

As he did so for some time, Nola wondered if he had caught a chill when they were fishing.

The Earl wiped his lips with his handkerchief and said:

"I had a very bad cough when I was in the desert, perhaps from some of the very unpleasant weeds that are found there."

"Does it hurt you?" Nola asked.

"No, it is just somewhat rough and uncomfortable," the Earl replied.

"Then I will tell you what you must do," Nola said. "You must gargle with honey and also drink some last thing at night. It is something my Mother always recommended, and I have never known it fail."

"I will certainly try it," the Earl said.

At that moment Newman came in to put a log on the fire.

It was not cold at night, but a small fire seemed cheerful in the room.

"Oh, Newman," Nola said. "His Lordship has a bad cough. Will you put two teaspoonfuls of honey in a glass for him and fill it up with hot water. If he drinks it last thing, I am sure his throat will be better in the morning."

"It's what your Mother always recommended," Newman said, "and it's somethin' I've always taken myself if I've any trouble with me throat."

"There you are," Nola said to the Earl, "if Newman recommends it, I am sure you will be cured instantly."

"I am quite prepared to take your word for it," the Earl said. "I very much dislike this tickle which comes in my throat when I least expect it."

"I'll put the honey in Your Lordship's bedroom," Newman said.

"Thank you, Newman, and do not wait up for me. I will look after myself."

"Is Your Lordship quite sure?" Newman enquired.

"Quite sure," the Earl repeated.

Newman went from the room, and the Earl said to Nola:

"He has been valeting me because the footman you engaged has had no experience. However, he wants me to have a Valet, and I suppose sooner or later I shall have to get one."

"Of course you will now that you are so important," Nola said. "Otherwise how could you possibly dress and undress yourself?"

There was a slightly mocking note in her voice, and the Earl laughed.

"It is what I have done for twenty-seven years," he said, "but, of course, as you say, now that I am so very important, I expect everything to be done for me."

"And it will be!" Nola said.

It was sometime later before Harry and Gwen

came back from the Picture Gallery and Richard from outside.

"There is a moon tonight," he said. "I must say, Rollo, your garden, the lake, and the house itself look entrancing, as if it had all stepped out of a fairy story."

"That is exactly what it did," Nola said quietly.

She almost added, "reigned over by a fairy Prince."

She was still thinking of the Earl even though the conversation had changed to horses while they decided what they would all ride tomorrow morning.

"I think, as I have got to get up so early," Gwen said, "I would now like to go to bed."

"I will come with you," Nola said, "and I will call you at half-past six just in case you oversleep."

"I expect I shall be too excited to do that," Gwen answered, "but you had better make certain that I do not miss anything."

"Of course I will," Nola replied.

They said goodnight to the men.

Nola noticed that Harry actually kissed Gwen's cheek and whispered something which only she could hear.

"Do not be late tomorrow morning," the Earl admonished as they left the room.

They went up the stairs together, and Gwen said:

"I think he is charming, absolutely charming."

For a moment Nola thought she was speaking of the Earl, and then she realised it was Harry.

"He is very amusing," she said, "but do not let him break your heart."

There was a little smile on Gwen's face as she said softly:

"I would like him to try."

They reached the top of the stairs and Nola kissed Gwen goodnight.

"It is very exciting being here," she said. "I only hope it does not end too soon."

"That is exactly what I am thinking," Gwen answered. "Thank you, dearest Nola, for asking me to anything so thrilling."

She looked so pretty in the candlelight with her eyes shining like stars.

Nola thought it would be very strange if Harry or Richard did not fall in love with her.

It went through her mind that perhaps the Earl would also find her very attractive.

Then she was shocked at herself because she was jealous.

She went into her own room.

Soon after she had undressed and was brushing her hair, she heard the men coming up to bed.

The Earl was laughing at something Harry had said.

She thought how young, carefree, and happy they sounded.

When she said her prayers, she prayed once again that the Earl would be safe, and Basil would not be able to hurt him.

As she got into bed she hoped he had remembered to drink the honey.

She wished she had made sure it was there before she went to her own room.

It was then she remembered something.

While she and Gwen were coming up the stairs, she had seen one of the footmen move along the corridor.

He was coming from the direction of the Master Suite.

She supposed Newman, having made the honey as she requested, had told him to put it in the Earl's room.

Then she thought that surely Newman would have taken it himself.

He would have gone to the Master Suite to put the Earl's night clothes ready for him.

The footman she had seen moving along the corridor had been a dark-haired young man whose family had only recently come to the village.

In fact, she knew very much less about him than the other footmen she had found for Newman.

They had all come from families who had lived in the village for many years.

She turned over in bed and shut her eyes.

Then suddenly, as if like a ghost coming to haunt her, her brain was talking to her.

That particular footman was unlikely to have gone to the Earl's bedroom on Newman's instructions.

If it was not on his instructions, why was he there?

She found the question turning itself over and over in her mind.

It suddenly struck her that Basil would try anything to destroy the Earl, so why not poison?

He had bribed Betsy to open the door for him.

Why should he not have bribed Alan to put something in the Earl's drink.

What could be more convenient than a glass of honey in his bedroom?

Because she was frightened, Nola sat up in bed.

Then, as if it were a picture in front of her eyes, she could see the Earl undressing.

Then he was drinking the honey which she had told him would cure his cough.

It would not be a deadly poison which would have been put into it.

That would kill him and it would be easy to

trace from the footman to Basil.

He had an undoubted reason for wishing his Cousin dead.

No, it would have to be something more subtle than that.

Again, like a picture in front of her eyes, she could see the Earl sleeping soundly.

What he had just drunk was a sleeping drug.

What then?

Clearly and distinctly she could hear the Earl saying of his Cousin:

"He has been extremely athletic all his life. He prides himself on being able to climb the highest mountains we have in this country and is, I believe, one of the first men to climb Mont Blanc."

As the words came to her, Nola jumped out of bed.

She put on her pretty lace-trimmed dressing gown which was lying on the chair.

Then, going to the door, she opened it very quietly.

There was no-one in the corridor and everything was very quiet.

She moved towards the Master Suite.

As she had not put on her slippers, she made no sound on the thick carpet.

When she reached the door to the Master Suite, she hesitated.

Then she told herself that if the Earl were drugged, he would not know that she was there.

She had to save him from what his Cousin intended.

She opened the door.

The room might have been in darkness, but the Earl must have pulled back the curtains before he got into bed.

The moonlight which Richard had admired filled the room with a silver light.

Nola could see quite clearly.

The Earl was asleep in the huge four-poster bed with its heavy velvet curtains on either side of it.

Then she looked across the room and saw the middle window was wide open.

She stood very still, looking at the window, thinking perhaps she was imagining what might happen.

Then she heard a sound.

It was only a very soft sound, yet it was definitely coming from outside the window.

It was not a sound one might expect in the middle of the night.

Now she was listening intently without moving.

The sound came again, so faint, yet it was definitely there.

Then she knew, almost as if someone had told her, that Basil, who could climb mountains, was climbing up the outside of the house.

She knew then exactly what he intended to do.

Alan had been bribed, perhaps, to put a sleeping powder in something the Earl drank.

When he was sleeping and unconscious of what was happening, Basil would climb into his room.

He would hold a pillow over the Earl's face.

In the morning there would be no sign of the Earl being suffocated.

He would merely be found dead when Newman called him and Basil would be the 7th Earl of Hallington.

It all swept through Nola's mind as if she were watching the slides on a magic lantern.

Then the sound came again, a little nearer and a little louder.

She knew what she must do.

Slowly and absolutely soundlessly she moved across the room.

As she reached the window she stooped down so that her head would not be seen above the ledge.

Now she was well aware of Basil climbing up outside.

She could hear each movement he made and knew he was only a few feet from the open window.

"Help me, God . . . help . . . me," Nola prayed.

Now the sound was nearer still.

Then, just above her eyes, she saw his fingers against the brick ledge outside the window.

It was then she lifted up her arms.

With a violent movement, using all her strength, she pulled the window shut.

As she did so, making a noise like an explosion, there was a scream from outside, followed by another.

Nola stood up and put her hands over her eyes.

Then, to her astonishment, she heard a voice ask:

"What the Devil is happening?"

It was the Earl who spoke, and he was sitting up in bed.

She stared at him for a moment.

Then she covered her eyes with her hands again.

"I . . . have . . . killed . . . him," she said incoherently, "I . . . have killed . . . him."

chapter seven

THE Earl jumped out of bed.

Picking up his dark robe which was lying over a chair, he pulled it on as he came towards Nola.

"What has happened?" he asked as he reached her.

She did not take her hands from her face, but murmured:

"He was . . . climbing . . . up to . . . kill you. I know . . . that is . . . what he . . . meant to do."

The Earl turned towards the window and pulled it open.

He bent forward.

In the moonlight he could see his Cousin Basil stretched out on the ground below.

He did not appear to be capable of moving.

The Earl was wondering what he should do, when there was a sound of horses' hooves.

Coming up the drive and crossing the bridge was a closed carriage drawn by two horses.

It was travelling at a tremendous pace.

The horses were drawn up sharply just as they reached the courtyard.

Two men jumped out of the carriage.

They picked up Basil, one by the shoulders and the other by the feet.

They carried him at a run across the gravel and placed him in the back of the carriage.

Then the man driving turned the horses round and they left at the same pace at which they had arrived.

It all happened so swiftly that the Earl had no time to take in details of the carriage or the men in it.

Almost before he could realise what was happening, it had disappeared under the oak trees in the drive.

He turned back to where Nola was still standing.

He put his arms around her as if to support her.

"He was ... climbing in ... so that he ... could suffocate ... you," she said in a voice he could hardly hear. "I knew that ... was what ... he intended ... to do."

"And you have saved me once again," the Earl said gently.

"But I ... killed him," she whispered. "Was ... that very ... very ... wrong of ... me?"

She looked up at him, and now in the moonlight he could see the tears in her eyes.

He realised as he held her that she was trembling.

"You saved me," he said quietly, "as you saved me before, and that, as you know, was the right thing to do."

He thought she still looked anxious and at the same time very pathetic.

Then, as she tried to speak, no words came to her lips.

He bent his head and kissed her.

It was a very gentle kiss, and yet to Nola it was as if the stars had fallen from the sky and she was enveloped with them.

She had never been kissed before.

It could not be true that the Earl, of all people, had kissed her!

Yet her whole body responded to it in a strange manner she did not understand.

Instinctively she drew a little closer to him, and then his lips became more possessive.

She felt as if the moonlight were shining not only on them from the sky, but was in her heart and in his too.

The Earl kissed her for what seemed a long time.

Then he raised his head, saying in a deep voice which was somehow a little unsteady.

"How could you be so brave? How could you know that Basil had thought of yet another way of destroying me?"

"I am sure . . . he had . . . paid one of the . . . footmen to drug you," she said, "and I . . . thought it was in . . . the honey that New-man . . . made for . . . you."

The Earl smiled.

"I must confess," he said, "that I forgot to drink it."

"Then I knew," Nola said, "that Alan, who I saw coming from your . . . room, had . . . put some sort . . . of sleeping drug . . . in it."

"Nothing would surprise me," the Earl said. "But you were aware that having, as he thought, drugged me, Basil was climbing up the house. How could you think of such a thing?"

"You told me that he . . . had climbed . . . moun-tains," Nola said. "I think it was . . . God who . . . meant me to . . . save you because . . . I felt some-one was . . . telling me what he . . . would do and that he would . . . suffocate you . . . while you were asleep."

The Earl's arms tightened round her.

"How could any human being think of anything so despicable?" he questioned.

"When I . . . shut . . . the window, he screamed," Nola said, "and . . . fell."

Now the fear and uncertainty was back in her voice.

"You are not to think of it again," the Earl said. "He has been picked up and taken away by, I suppose, the carriage which brought him here. If he dies, I shall doubtless be informed of it. If he lives, he will be able to try again."

"Oh! No . . . no!" Nola cried. "I cannot . . . bear it."

The Earl looked down at her.

"Would you really mind so much," he asked quietly, "if Basil did kill me?"

"You . . . know I . . . would," Nola replied.

"But why, what does it mean to you?"

She looked up into his eyes.

Then with a little murmur she turned her face and hid it against his shoulder.

"Tell me," he said very softly.

She did not reply, but he thought she shook her head.

"I want to know, Nola," he said, "why you would mind so much if I died?"

"How . . . could you die . . . when you have . . . so much . . . to do and so . . . many people . . . who depend . . . on you?"

"I am not concerned at the moment about other people," the Earl said, "only you. Tell me, my Darling, what you feel for me."

He felt her whole body stiffen for a moment at the endearment.

Then it seemed that she melted into him.

"Tell me," he said again.

"I . . . love . . . you."

"This is what I have hoped and prayed you would say," the Earl answered. "And I have loved you since the very first moment you were brave enough to tell me what was happening."

He smiled as he went on:

"But I knew you were hating me."

"How . . . could you . . . have known . . . that?" Nola enquired.

"I could see it in your eyes," he said. "I think, too, you resented the fact that I had been in Wolseley's Army which arrived in Khartoum three days too late."

Now Nola raised her head and looked up at the Earl in astonishment.

"How could . . . you possibly . . . know I felt . . . like that," she asked.

"Ever since I have known you," the Earl answered, "I have been able to read your thoughts. I cannot explain it even to myself, but I know what you are thinking. I knew that you resented me being alive when your hero, General Gordon, was dead."

"It was not . . . really quite . . . as bad . . . as that," Nola murmured.

"I think it was," the Earl answered. "And you were also angry with me for the parties I had given in London which I had no idea would be talked about here, and, of course, the party I brought down with me so that my friends could see my country house."

Because she felt shy at what he was saying, Nola's face was hidden in his shoulder.

Now the Earl put his fingers under her chin and turned her face up to his.

"I love you, my Darling," he said, "and I know, because you have looked after me like a Guardian Angel, that you love me. How soon can we be married?"

Nola gave a little gasp and stared at him.

"Are you . . . seriously asking . . . me to marry . . . you?"

"Very seriously," he answered. "I am telling you that I intend to marry you—and as soon as possible. I want you, I cannot live without you, and I love you, my Darling."

He did not wait for her to answer but pulled her closer still.

He kissed her possessively and passionately until they were both breathless.

He raised his head and looked at her.

He thought with the moonlight in her eyes it was impossible for anyone to look so lovely or so radiant.

Then he picked her up in his arms and, carrying her to the bed, laid her down against the pillows.

"We cannot go on talking about our future," he said, "and keep standing while we do so."

He lay down beside her on top of the bed and put his arms round her shoulders.

"Now tell me you love me," he said, "and I will tell you what we are going to do."

"I love . . . you with . . . all my . . . heart," Nola whispered.

"That is what I wanted you to say," the Earl said as he smiled. "When did you first know you loved me?"

Nola thought for a moment.

"I admitted it only today, but I think really I first loved you when you were so splendid in Church and delighted . . . all the village . . . exactly as I . . . wanted you to."

"And I wanted to please you," the Earl said.

"And the villagers," Nola added. "You mean so much to . . . them, they must . . . mean something . . . to you."

"They will mean what you want them to

mean," the Earl said. "It will be much easier once we are married."

Nola drew in her breath.

"Because I . . . love you . . . so much," she said in a very small voice, "I do not . . . think I . . . ought to . . . marry you."

"Why is that?" the Earl asked.

"Because you . . . heard what . . . Gwen said about the . . . Marchioness and all . . . the other Lings who . . . expect you to marry . . . someone very . . . important . . . who they can . . . admire as your Countess."

"They will admire you, my Darling, as soon as they know you," the Earl said. "But let me make it quite clear, I have no intention of marrying just to please the Marchioness or anyone else. I have always sworn to myself that I would never marry anyone until I was completely and absolutely in love. And I swear to you on everything you hold sacred that I have never been in love until now."

Nola had a quick thought of the *Contessa*.

As if once again he were reading her thoughts, the Earl said:

"Forget her! She was just part of the amusements in London which I have never encountered before and I have no particular wish to encounter again."

He kissed her cheek and said:

"What really interests me and what I want more than anything else is you, my Darling. We have so many exciting and thrilling things to do together."

"You are sure . . . you are . . . quite sure . . . that you do not . . . mind that I am . . . just the Vicar's daughter?"

"The most adorable, the most beautiful, and the most enchanting Vicar's daughter that has ever been," the Earl said. "In fact, when the Social

World meets you, I suspect it will suddenly become the fashion for Peers to marry their Vicar's daughters."

Nola laughed.

"You are . . . making a . . . joke of it. But you are very . . . very . . . important, and as . . . doubtless the Marchioness will tell you when . . . she arrives, you must do . . . your duty to your . . . family and your . . . country."

"I am not afraid of the Marchioness or anyone else," the Earl said. "Quite frankly, my Precious, I intend to have my own way and marry as quickly as possible before all the arguments for and against my marriage begin."

"What are . . . we to do . . . about . . . Basil?" Nola said in a very small voice.

"I have already told you," the Earl said, "there is nothing we can do at the moment. He obviously came here, as you clearly and brilliantly anticipated, to kill me by suffocation or some other means while I was drugged into unconsciousness."

The Earl hesitated, as if he were thinking before he continued:

"He came in a very fast carriage, and I am sure he intended, when he had commited the murder, to drive away for some distance, so there was no possibility of him being connected in any way with my death."

"I had not . . . thought of . . . that . . . before," Nola said, "but now it . . . seems as if it . . . would have . . . been the . . . sensible thing . . . to do."

"Of course it would," the Earl said, "and his friends or employees or whoever was with him were merely carrying out his orders when they picked him up off the ground and drove away as swiftly as was possible."

"If he . . . lives." Nola said as if she were speaking to herself, "he . . . will try . . . again."

"But you will be with me," the Earl said, pulling her closer, "and, my Precious, as my Guardian Angel, you will save me as you have saved me already."

"I can only . . . pray that I . . . shall be . . . able to do . . . so," Nola said.

"How can you doubt it, when you have been so successful already?" the Earl enquired. "Let us go back for a moment. You said that you fell in love with me in Church and that was the third day after we had met."

He held up one hand as he went on:

"The number three seems to come into everything that concerns us both. You hated me because Wolseley was three days too late to save Gordon. I was born three days before Basil, which was why he has been trying to murder me. Now you tell me that you loved me three days after we met."

He smiled before he finished.

"We will therefore be married, my Darling, in three days, which will be Thursday. That gives me time to get a Special Licence and also arrange our wedding and our honeymoon."

Nola had been listening to him almost as if she were mesmerised by what he was saying.

Now she gave a little cry.

"I must be . . . married . . . by Papa," she said. "I could not do it behind his back. He would . . . never forgive me."

"Then we must get in touch with him and find out what is happening," the Earl said, "because I do not intend, my Darling, to wait any longer than three days for you."

He was thinking that when Nola learned that Basil was dead, she would be upset.

It might be even worse to know that he was alive.

Once again they would both have to be on their guard.

"I must be with her, and protect her," the Earl was saying in his heart.

He knew it was something he had never felt for any woman before.

Then he bent over and kissed her.

It was a long, passionate kiss which made her feel the stars that had enveloped her before were all twinkling inside her breast.

"Now I am going to send you to bed, my Precious," the Earl said. "Tomorrow no-one in the house must know what has happened here tonight and we must behave as if we are both completely carefree."

"Oh! I love ... you, I love ... you," Nola said. "How could you be ... so marvellous? How could I ... ever have thought for ... a moment that you were not ... exactly the right person to be ... the Earl of Hallington?"

"I still have a long way to go to live up to what you expect of me," the Earl said, "and the sooner we get on with it the better."

He sat up on the bed as he spoke.

Then, as he looked at Nola in the moonlight coming through the window, he said:

"What I want to do is to keep you here all night, telling you how much I love you. But we have to go back to propriety for at least the next three days."

She smiled at him and put out her hand towards him.

"I love you," he said in a very deep voice. "You are not to tempt me into doing anything which I think would shock you."

"I suppose we should not really be sitting on this bed," Nola said.

The Earl gave a little laugh.

"That is another secret between us, my Precious. I have so much to teach you about love, and it is going to be the most exciting thing I have ever done."

He pulled her to her feet and held her very close against him. Then he said:

"Go to bed, my Darling. It is going to be difficult for me to sleep when all I can think of is how beautiful you are and how much I want you with me. But I promise I will wait three days."

Nola hoped it would not have to be longer than that, although she did not say so.

Instead, she let the Earl take her to the door.

As if he could not help himself, he swept her into his arms.

He kissed her until she felt as if the whole house were whirling round her and they were both flying into the sky.

She clung to him, finding it impossible to think, only to feel the wonder and ecstasy of him.

He took her outside the door of the Master Suite.

"Goodnight, my Precious little wife-to-be," he murmured, and his voice was unsteady.

Then she found herself alone in the corridor.

She knew he was taking every precaution just in case anyone should see her coming from his room.

She hurried to her own.

Her bed was as she had left it, with just the candles a little lower.

She thought what had happened must be a dream and not reality.

But it was true.

By some miraculous way which could have

come only from God she had managed to save the Earl.

Otherwise tomorrow she would have been woken to be told that he had died in his sleep.

No-one except herself would have ever attributed his death to Basil!

She got into bed feeling as if in the short time she had been away her whole world had changed.

The Earl loved her and wanted to marry her.

She loved him and her whole body was pulsating with the wonder and glory of his kisses.

'I love . . . him, I love . . . him,' she thought.

Now, because he loved her, the words seemed to be accompanied by a soft music that could have come from only Heaven itself.

Nola woke and realised it was nearly half-past six.

Then the events of the last night flooded over her.

She did not feel tired or sleepy. She felt only as if the Life Force itself was pulsating through her body.

She jumped out of bed and ran first to Gwen's room to knock on the door.

She heard Gwen murmur "come in," but she just said:

"It is six thirty," and ran back to her own room.

She dressed quickly and at the same time she looked in the mirror, wanting to look beautiful for the Earl.

She could not help thinking that she had never seen herself look so radiant or so ecstatically happy.

"I . . . love him," she told her own reflection.

She found the Earl already in the stables.

When their eyes met for a moment, neither of them could move.

Then the Earl said in a voice only she could hear:

"Are you all right?"

"Very, very happy," Nola replied.

Harry was already choosing the horse he intended to ride and being fussy over which one was good enough for Gwen.

Nola wished that she and the Earl could be riding alone.

At the same time, she was thanking God that he was there and not lying immobile in his bed as Basil had intended.

Their horses were nearly ready by the time Richard joined them.

"You are late," Harry said.

"I know," Richard replied. "I had difficulty in waking myself up. It is all Rollo's fault for giving us such good wine at dinner."

"You did not have to drink it," the Earl replied laughingly.

As he spoke, Nola thought how fortunate it was that he had forgotten to drink the honey which Newman had prepared for him.

Later on she got the chance, when she and the Earl were out of earshot of the others, to ask:

"What are you going to do about Alan?"

"I think it would be a mistake to ask any questions," the Earl replied, "although I am quite certain that Basil must have bribed him."

"Did you look at the honey? Was there anything in the glass?" Nola asked.

"It was a slightly strange colour and rather thicker than it should have been," the Earl said.

"And you threw it away?" Nola asked.

"I tipped it out of the window," the Earl replied. "I did not want anyone realising I had not drunk it, or, as far as the footmen were concerned, believing that it had affected me in any way."

141

Nola thought this was very sensible and wise of him.

At the same time, she wondered if they would ever be free of the worry, the difficulties, and the lies that Basil had forced upon them.

They rode for a long time, and it made breakfast much later than usual.

Then they went off to inspect the jumps that the Earl had ordered to be made and try out those that were finished.

It made the morning pass quite amusingly.

At the same time, Nola could not help wondering if they would hear about Basil and how soon it might be before they did so.

Because the Earl knew what she was feeling, he said, when they were riding from one side of the ground to the other:

"Stop worrying."

"How do you know I am worrying?" Nola replied.

"I know everything about you," he said. "What you are thinking, what you are feeling, and how much you are loving me."

She smiled at him.

"That is a great deal, and it is going to be a great deal more."

"My resolution is not as you might think," the Earl replied, "to finish making the jumps or to construct, as Harry wants, a race-course which will out-vie Newmarket, Ascot, and Epsom, but just to make you love me."

Nola blushed a little.

At the same time, her eyes lit up in a way which the Earl found entrancing.

Most of the afternoon he was thinking of things he could say to her which would bring that same light into her eyes.

It gave a radiance to her face he had never seen in any other woman.

It had something spiritual about it which moved him very deeply.

He knew that he was falling more and more in love with her every moment they were together.

He was only afraid that their happiness might be spoilt when there was news of Basil.

But he was sensible enough to realise it might be days or weeks before they would learn where he was and what condition he was in.

Harry was plying the Earl with suggestions as to the jumps and the race-course.

"The more I think about it, Rollo," he said, "you realise this is exactly the place where a race-course is wanted. There is nothing in the County to attract men who are keen on horses, and what you will have to start in the winter is a really tip-top pack of fox hounds."

"If you give me many more things to do," the Earl protested, "I shall be working from dawn to dusk with no time to enjoy myself."

"You will enjoy yourself when you have got everything settled," Harry replied.

"As you are so keen on it all," the Earl said, "I think we had better go into partnership. I shall certainly need help—and experienced help at that."

"That is a good idea," Harry said, "I shall certainly consider it."

"Well, I think you should accept," Gwen said.

Harry looked at her.

"Of course," he said, "you conveniently have a house nearby. Perhaps we could use it when the time comes as a place to house the more important of our guests."

Gwen held up her hands in horror.

"I do not want to be involved in that way," she said.

"Well, I will think of another," Harry said, "but I have every intention of you being involved."

He spoke with a meaning in his voice which made Nola look at him.

It suddenly occurred to her it would be very happy for Gwen if she and Harry were in love with each other.

They certainly seemed to have a lot to say as they rode over the ground.

But she was half afraid that Harry was merely flirting with Gwen.

Perhaps he would in a day or two go back to London, where undoubtedly Lady Edith would be waiting for him.

"You are looking worried again," the Earl said accusingly. "What is upsetting you?"

"I am just hoping that Harry and Gwen might fall in love with each other," Nola said.

The Earl looked surprised, then he said:

"Why not? It is time Harry settled down, and I think Gwen is charming and as it happens very intelligent."

"Perhaps we can give some of our magic to them," Nola said in a low voice.

"We can try," the Earl agreed, "but at the same time, I want your magic, my Darling, all for myself. I shall be very jealous if you take too much interest in anyone else."

Nola laughed.

"You are quite safe at the moment," she said. "Remember, I have been used to a very quiet life at the Vicarage."

"I have not forgotten that," the Earl said. "But I know as soon as I take you to London you will be an instant success, acclaimed as a beauty, and have a dozen men like Harry running after you, telling you to forget me."

"You really think that is something I could do?" Nola asked.

"If you dare to even smile at anyone in the same way as you smile at me," he said, "I shall shut you up here and refuse to entertain anyone. There will just be you, me, and the horses, and you will never have a chance of flirting with anyone else."

"I can imagine nothing more wonderful," Nola said. "If you think I want to flirt like those exotic painted ladies you had to stay last week, you are very much mistaken."

"I know that," the Earl said, "but I love you, my Darling, exactly as you are, and I do not want you to change, now or ever."

"I will try not to," Nola said, "but, of course, as I get older, I hope I will get wiser."

"You are too clever already," the Earl said, "and I want you just as you are."

They smiled at each other.

As he glanced at her lips, Nola knew he was wanting to kiss her.

"I am the luckiest person in the world," she told herself.

They arrived back at the house late for tea.

Newman pointed out that if they were not careful, they would spoil the dinner which Mrs. Newman was planning with great care.

"All the same," Richard said when he left the room, "I cannot resist these scones. It is something I can never get in London. And that reminds me, Rollo, I have to go back tomorrow. I have got a very important meeting with my Solicitor and I cannot put him off as I have done twice already."

"Then you must come back again as soon as you can," the Earl said. "I suppose even the best parties cannot go on forever."

He glanced at Harry as he spoke, who said:

"If you are suggesting it is time I left, Rollo, I think I should tell you that it is impossible for you to be rid of me."

The Earl looked at him, not quite understanding, and he went on:

"There is so much to do here, and Gwen has promised to help me, and we thought the sooner we got married the better."

The Earl gave an exclamation of astonishment, and Nola jumped up to kiss Gwen.

"I am so glad, Dearest," she said.

"I fell in love with Harry the moment I saw him," Gwen responded, "and by a strange coincidence he did the same thing with me."

"I have been looking for her all my life," Harry said, "and when she walked into the room, something inside me said, 'Here she is,' so loudly, I thought you would all hear."

The Earl laughed.

"It is the best news I have ever heard, and of course we will all celebrate. I think, as we have just had tea, we should keep the Champagne until dinner time."

"What we plan to do," Harry said, "is to help you with your race-course, and I will move into Gwen's house while we are doing it. You know that my home in the country is very dilapidated. Because it always bored me to be there alone after my Father died, it wants a great deal doing to it. Gwen and I thought we would do that later."

"What he really said," Gwen told Nola later, "is that we will go back there when we have a family."

"Oh! Dearest, that is exactly what I want for you, and I like Harry so much," Nola said.

"How could I know," Gwen asked, "when I

was so lonely and rather sad, that you would come like a messenger from the Gods to ask me to chaperon you? It was the most marvellous thing I ever did, and I hope one day, Dearest, you will be as happy as me."

Nola wanted to tell her that she was ecstatically happy at that moment, but thought she must just ask the Earl if they could confide in their two friends.

She and Gwen put on their prettiest dresses for dinner.

They knew that the Earl would be seeking in the cellar for the finest wine in which to drink the health of the newly engaged couple.

They met a little later than usual in the Drawing-Room.

The Earl was just handing Nola a glass of Champagne when the door opened and a voice said:

"May I come in? There was no-one in the hall, but I am told my daughter is here."

Nola gave a cry."

"Papa!"

It was her Father.

Putting down her glass, she ran across to him.

"Papa, you are back! I was wondering when we would hear from you."

The Vicar kissed her.

"You must forgive me. I have been so busy since I left and did not have a moment to write to you. But now I am home to find that you are here at the Hall."

"I have a lot to tell you, Papa," Nola said. "But first you must meet the new Earl."

He was walking towards her as he spoke and held out his hand to the Vicar.

"I am delighted to meet you," he said. "Nola

will tell you later about the great number of things which have happened since you left."

"I heard from Nanny there was great excitement over your arrival," the Vicar said.

As he spoke, he saw Gwen Castleford and went towards her.

"I did not expect to find you here, Gwen," he said. "It is delightful to see you again."

"I am chaperoning Nola," Gwen replied, "and as it happens having a very wonderful time."

She glanced at Harry as she spoke, and the Earl said:

"Let me introduce Lord Longdon, who is one of my oldest friends, and, as I expect you have realised by this time, Harry, this is Nola's Father, the Reverend Mr. Brackley."

The Vicar shook Harry's hand and then he said:

"I think I should explain to my daughter that my name now is Brackleydale."

Nola stared at him in astonishment, and then she said:

"I never thought of that! So now that your brother is dead, you have come into the title."

"Of course," her Father said. "Because, although my brother produced four daughters, there was no son."

"What you are saying," Gwen interposed, "is that you are now Lord Brackleydale. Oh! I am so glad. It is much more glamorous than being just Mr. Brackley."

The Vicar laughed.

"I am glad you think so. But at the same time my life has turned upside down upside down in a way I did not expect."

"Why, Papa, what has happened apart from that?" Nola asked.

"Well, my Dearest," the Vicar said, "I have inherited not only my brother's title, but also the family home and Estate which is far larger than I remembered. I am afraid that His Lordship will have to find a new Vicar for the Hall and also a new private Chaplain."

"I did not realise I had one," the Earl said. "But before you leave Hallington, I think I should tell you that you will be leaving your daughter behind."

The Vicar looked at the Earl for a moment in perplexity.

Then, as the Earl moved closer to him, the Vicar said:

"Are you saying what I think you are?"

"I am saying," the Earl interrupted, "that Nola has promised to marry me and to make me the happiest man that ever existed."

The Vicar stared from one to the other, and then he said:

"This is certainly a surprise."

"I am so happy, Papa," Nola said. "I am sure you will love Rollo as I do when you know him."

"I am sure I shall," the Vicar said. "May I say I am delighted to greet you as my future son-in-law."

They shook hands, then Gwen gave a cry.

"You did not tell me. Oh! Darling Nola, I am so happy for you. Just as I am so happy to be marrying Harry."

By the time everyone had congratulated each other, it was only left to Richard to say:

"Well, I am certainly the odd man out. I think quite frankly I shall marry one of Rollo's finest mares and the least he can do is to give her to me as a wedding present."

They all laughed at this.

When they went into dinner, there was so much to talk about, it was difficult for anyone to get a word in edgeways.

It was finally arranged that the Earl would send

his Secretary to London to get two Special Licences the following day.

The Vicar promised to marry first his daughter and the Earl, and afterwards Gwen and Harry.

"What about your family?" Gwen asked a little anxiously.

"They have never troubled themselves much with me," Harry replied. "I see no reason why we should hold up the marriage to make it one of those boring social occasions which I have always avoided with great dexterity."

"You will be married here," the Earl said. "I am quite certain Nola is going to tell me that I must include the whole Estate in my marriage festivities, and that is exactly what I will do."

Nola looked at him with shining eyes, and he went on:

"They will have the fireworks they enjoyed on Guy Fawkes' Day, as much ale as they can tip down their throats, and, of course, after we have left, the lake must be lit up and the house as well so that they can dance and sing until the early hours of the morning."

Nola clapped her hands together.

"Only you could think of anything so clever," she said. "It will delight them and give them something to talk about for the next thousand years."

"That is what I thought," the Earl said.

"Let us have two weddings on the same day," Harry said. "You can have yours first, and, of course, be covered in rice and rose petals, and Gwen and I will be married after the Church has emptied and start our honeymoon in her house, where we can be alone."

He glanced at Gwen as he spoke.

As their eyes met, Nola, watching them, knew they were very much in love and as happy as she was.

"How could everything turn out so wonder-fully?" she asked.

She knew she would thank God when she said her prayers later.

They had so much to plan that it was late when they went to bed.

The Vicar insisted on returning to his own house because he said Nanny would be waiting for him.

He promised to be back in the morning.

When he had gone, Nola walked upstairs with the Earl beside her.

Harry and Gwen went back into the Drawing-Room.

When Nola reached her room, she said:

"Could anything be more wonderful?"

"Yes, it will be," the Earl replied, "when I ac-tually marry you, my Darling, then I will not have to say 'goodnight' as I must do now."

He pulled her against him almost roughly and kissed her, not gently, but with fierce, demanding kisses which told her how much he loved her.

"I want you," he said, "and every minute you are not with me makes me want you almost un-bearably."

"You do not think ... anything could ... pos-sibly keep us from ... being married ... next Thursday?" Nola asked.

The Earl knew she was thinking that perhaps in some extraordinary way Basil would interfere with their plans.

"Nothing," he said firmly. "I will not have you worrying, my Darling. Now, you go to sleep and dream of me as I shall be dreaming of you."

He kissed her again.

Then he went abruptly from the room as he forced himself to leave.

Nola shut her eyes.

"How could I be so lucky to feel like this and know that Rollo feels the same?" she asked. "Please, please, dear God, do . . . not let . . . anything spoil it."

There was so much to arrange in the next two days that Nola thought afterwards she could only remember being almost breathless.

She and Gwen went off to the nearest town.

They managed to buy a great many things, including a pretty white gown for Nola.

"If you wear that," Gwen said, "with the veil that has been worn by all the Countesses of Hallington for generations, and, of course, some of the Hallington diamonds, you will look marvellous."

Because she herself had been married before, she was not being married in white.

They found instead a very pretty pale blue dress which matched her eyes.

"Harry says he likes me in blue," she said.

There was no question therefore of her choosing anything else.

It was the Earl who saw to everything.

He sent someone to fetch the fireworks from the nearest town.

He ordered the gardeners to make the Church a bower of beauty.

He planned the most delicious food for everyone from the village to eat in the marquees that were erected on the lawns.

There were also large barrels of ale which were traditional.

The fairy lights arrived for the lake and were also arranged over the lintels of the windows.

Nola knew how beautiful it would look when darkness came.

"It is rather sad we will not see it," she said to the Earl.

He smiled and then he said:

"I will let you into a secret—we will."

"What do you mean? You said we were going away on our honeymoon!"

"I thought it over," he said, "and I have decided it would be less exhausting and also happier if we started our honeymoon here. But no-one must know about it."

"How will we manage that?" Nola asked.

"We will ride away in an open carriage—seen, of course, by the whole village. Then only Groves, who will be driving the carriage, will be in on the secret. He will bring us round the lanes and though the paddock to the stables. We will slip into the house when they will all be dancing and singing and go up to our own room. There, I think, my Darling, we will be more comfortable and happier than anywhere else."

"Oh, I will," Nola said, "because this house means so much to me. It has been part of my childhood, my growing up, and then, of course . . . you.

"That is what I thought," the Earl said. "Do not forget, my lovely one, that it is a secret and no-one must know that we have not gone to Paris or some other part of the world that could not mean for one moment as much as Hallington Hall means to us."

"You are so clever," Nola said.

Then, as he was kissing her, she could not say any more.

Everything went exactly according to plan.

Nola came up the aisle on Harry's arm.

The Earl thought when he saw her that it was impossible for any bride to look more lovely or more radiant.

The Church was, as he had planned, filled with flowers and fragrant with the scent of them.

All the village was there to see them married, with Nanny and Gwen sitting in the front pew.

"There were no disagreeable relatives," Nola said later, "to protest that Rollo might have done better."

There were only the people who loved and admired them.

They thought that their wedding was the most exciting that had ever happened.

The Vicar read the service with sincerity and love.

It made Nola feel that her Mother was beside him and as pleased as he was that their daughter had found real love as they had done.

When Nola and the Earl knelt for the Blessing, she was sure her Mother was blessing them too.

'We will never lose the love we feel for each other,' Nola thought.

They drove back to the Hall with the village children running beside them.

They cheered and threw flowers into the carriage.

They moved amongst pensioners, farmers, and all the people who had known Nola since she was a baby.

After the huge cake had been cut and he had made a speech, the Earl said it was time to leave.

Nola went upstairs to take off her beautiful Brussels lace veil and the diamond tiara which held it in place.

The Earl changed and they went downstairs hand in hand.

The open carriage was waiting for them.

There were no footmen on the box, only Groves, driving two outstanding carriage horses.

They had garlands of flowers around their necks.

Flowers decorated the hood that was laid back on the carriage behind the bride and bridegroom.

Everyone had gathered in the courtyard to say goodbye.

A shower of rose petals covered them as they stepped into the carriage.

Everyone was cheering and waving as they set off down the drive.

Nola slipped her hand in the Earl's.

She knew by the expression on his face that he had enjoyed the love he felt flowing out of the people she had known all her life as much as she had.

To Nola it was all enchanting.

What she did not know was that just before the Earl had left for the Church, he had received a letter.

It had been brought to him by messenger.

When Newman brought it to him on a silver salver, he looked at it apprehensively.

He felt it contained something important and was afraid it might spoil his wedding.

"The messenger's waiting, M'Lord," Newman said.

He withdrew from the room as he spoke, but the Earl knew he was waiting outside.

For a moment he hesitated, thinking he would leave the letter until later in case it contained bad news.

Then he forced himself to open it.

The letter was headed with the name of a Doctor Grayson of whom he had never heard.

He saw from the inscribed address that he lived in a village some fifteen miles away.

The Earl drew in his breath and read:

"My Lord.
Very late on Monday night a gentleman was

brought to my house by two men who informed me he had hired their carriage and horses with instructions, after he had visited a certain house, to take him to the Posting-Inn in this village.

They told me, however, that he had met with an accident and been knocked unconscious. They had therefore brought him to me, thinking it the most sensible thing to do.

I discovered the gentleman had broken a number of bones, including his spine.

The men had not specified in what type of accident he had been involved. I treated him to the best of my ability, but unfortunately, without gaining consciousness, he died in the early hours of the following morning.

As they left no name, nor did he have any address on him, he was buried in the Churchyard at the expense of the village.

I tried to get in touch with the two men who had brought him to me and learned they had come from London and only hired the Chaise.

I felt there was nothing I could do until quite by chance I found, after he was buried, that his underclothes had a name on them in the same way that boys at school have their clothes marked.

The name in question was B. Ling.

I seem to have heard the name in the past, and the Proprietor of the Posting-Inn told me that you, as the Earl of Hallington, were the head of the Ling family.

I am therefore writing to you, My Lord, to inform you of what happened, and I hope this communication will be of interest to you.

I remain, My Lord,
　　Yours respectfully,
　　　E. Grayson."

The Earl read the letter carefully.

Then he knew that nothing could be a better present on his wedding day.

First, that Basil had lived after the fall.

If he broke the news gently to Nola, she would not be so acutely aware that she was responsible for his death.

Secondly, that the whole drama was now over.

Basil could no longer threaten them and Nola would no longer be afraid.

He put the letter in his pocket.

He did not intend to show it to Nola until they had been married for some days.

He would, of course, write to the Doctor to thank him for his attention to Basil and pay him for the trouble he had taken over him.

He would also say he had not the slightest idea how he had met with such an accident and could only be concerned that it had happened.

It was a precise and very excellent end to what he could think of as only an unpleasant and unnecessary drama in his life.

As the Earl and his wife passed the Church, they were both aware that at this moment Gwen and Harry were being married.

"Are you quite certain you do not mind us not staying to be at your wedding?" Nola had asked.

"Harry wants us just to be alone," Gwen answered, "except for Richard as a witness and an old aunt who lives in the same village as I do and who was thrilled to be asked."

Nola understood.

Harry had always been with what was thought

157

of as the "fast ladies," in London.

His friends were noisy men who had been at the first dinner party at the Hall.

Therefore, he wanted his wedding to Gwen to be quite different, just as their life together in the future would be very different to his previous life.

She just said a little prayer as they passed the church.

Groves took them down the small narrow lanes.

Fortunately it was dry, so he drove the carriage across the paddock and back into the stable yard.

Now they could hear the music coming from a Band playing on the lawn.

As the sun was sinking, Nola knew it would soon be time for the fireworks.

She and the Earl slipped in at the back door.

There was no-one in the kitchens as they passed them or the pantries.

Everyone was on the lawn, enjoying the festivities.

When they went upstairs, the house itself was very quiet.

To Nola's surprise, they did not go into the Master bedroom as she expected.

Instead, the Earl took her to another room.

She knew when she entered it that it was the one that had always been used by Countesses of Hallington.

It adjoined the Master Suite but looked out over the garden at the back.

As he opened the door, she was aware of the flowers which decorated the whole room, and the fragrance of them swept towards her.

"This is where we are staying tonight," the Earl said, "and we have a cold dinner arranged for us in the Boudoir where, my Darling, I will wait on you and we shall not be disturbed."

Nola thought afterwards that nothing could have been more romantic.

They dined alone on the most delicious dishes which the Earl offered her and kissed her between every course.

Vaguely in the distance they could hear the music of the Band.

By the time they had finished dinner, the fireworks were over.

The music seemed somewhat part of the fairy-tale atmosphere which surrounded everything they did and everything they said.

When finally Rollo took her into the next room, he lit only two candles by the bed.

Then he said:

"As there is no ladies'-maid, my Darling, I will help you to undress."

"I think that will make me shy," Nola said, and hid her face against his shoulder.

He kissed her hair, her forehead, her eyes, and then her lips.

She felt him undo the back of her gown, and as it slipped to the ground he lifted her up in his arms.

He carried her to the four-poster bed with its muslin curtains and splendidly carved posts of gold and silver.

He had drawn back the curtains, and through the open window Nola could see the stars overhead.

She felt, as she had felt before, that they were also twinkling in her breast.

Everything was so beautiful, and the fragrance seemed somehow part of their love.

Then Rollo joined her.

As he got into bed he pulled her close against him.

"Now at last," he said, "you are mine as I

meant you to be the first time I saw you, but I was so afraid I might lose you."

"I love you," Nola said.

As he did not answer, she said:

"Every day I think it is impossible to love you more. Every night I know that I do love you more than before and I feel it will go on forever."

"It will," the Earl promised.

The he was kissing her, at first very gently, his lips holding her captive.

Then he kissed her as he had before.

Her hair, her forehead, her eyes, her cheeks, and the softness of her neck.

She felt what she had never thought herself capable of feeling.

It was an ecstasy and a rapture that was beyond words and almost beyond thought.

As the Earl's hand touched her, he felt her body tremble and quiver beneath him.

Then he made Nola his.

They were both caught up in an ecstasy that was not magical but part of the Divine.

They not only reached the stars but entered together into a Heaven which was part of God.

It was theirs for their lives and for the Eternity which exists beyond it.

ABOUT THE AUTHOR

Barbara Cartland, the world's most famous romantic novelist, who is also an historian, playwright, lecturer, political speaker and television personality, has now written 623 books and sold over six hundred and twenty million copies all over the world.

She has also had many historical works published and has written four autobiographies as well as the biographies of her mother and that of her brother, Ronald Cartland, who was the first Member of Parliament to be killed in the last war. This book has a preface by Sir Winston Churchill and has been republished with an introduction by Sir Arthur Bryant.

Love at the Helm, a novel written with the help and inspiration of the late Earl Mountbatten of Burma, Great Uncle of His Royal Highness, The Prince of Wales, is being sold for the Mountbatten Memorial Trust.

She has broken the world record for the last twenty-one years by writing an average of twenty-three books a year. In the *Guinness Book of World Records* she is listed as the world's top-selling author.

Miss Cartland in 1987 sang an Album of Love Songs with the Royal Philharmonic Orchestra.

In private life Barbara Cartland, who is a Dame of the Order of St. John of Jerusalem and Chairman of the St. John Council in Hertfordshire, has fought for better conditions and salaries for Midwives and Nurses.

She championed the cause for the Elderly in 1956, invoking a Government Enquiry into the "Housing Condition of Old People."

In 1962 she had the Law of England changed so that Local Authorities had to provide camps for their own Gypsies. This has meant that since then thousands and thousands of Gypsy children have been able to go to School, which they had never been able to do in the past, as their caravans were moved every twenty-four hours by the Police.

There are now fifteen camps in Hertfordshire and Barbara Cartland has her own Romany Gypsy Camp called "Barbaraville" by the Gypsies.

Her designs "Decorating with Love" are being sold all over the U.S.A. and the National Home Fashions League made her, in 1981, "Woman of Achievement."

She is unique in that she was one and two in the Dalton list of Best Sellers, and one week had four books in the top twenty.

Barbara Cartland's book *Getting Older, Growing Younger* has been published in Great Britain and the U.S.A. and her fifth cookery book, *The Romance of Food*, is now being used by the House of Commons.

In 1984 she received, at Kennedy Airport, America's Bishop Wright Air Industry Award for her contribution to the development of aviation. In 1931 she and two R.A.F. Officers thought of, and carried, the first aeroplane-towed glider airmail.

During the War she was Chief Lady Welfare Officer in Bedfordshire, looking after 20,000 Servicemen and -women. She thought of having a pool of Wedding Dresses at the War Office so a Service Bride could hire a gown for the day.

She bought 1,000 gowns without coupons for the A.T.S., the W.A.A.F.s and the W.R.E.N.S. In 1945 Barbara Cartland received the Certificate of Merit from Eastern Command.

In 1964 Barbara Cartland founded the National Association for Health of which she is the President, as a front for all the Health Stores and for any product made as alternative medicine.

This is now a £65 million turnover a year, with one-third going in export.

In January 1968 she received *La Médeille de Vermeil de la Ville de Paris*. This is the highest award to be given in France by the City of Paris. She has sold 30 million books in France.

In March 1988 Barbara Cartland was asked by the Indian Government to open their Health Resort outside Delhi. This is almost the largest Health Resort in the world.

Barbara Cartland was received with great enthusiasm by her fans, who feted her at a reception in the City, and she received the gift of an embossed plate from the Government.

Barbara Cartland was made a Dame of the Order of the British Empire in the 1991 New Year's Honours List by Her Majesty, The Queen, for her contribution to Literature and also for her years of work for the community.

Dame Barbara has now written 623 books, the greatest number by a British author, passing the 564 books written by John Creasey.

AWARDS

1945   Received Certificate of Merit, Eastern Command, for being Welfare Officer to 5,000 troops in Bedfordshire.

1953   Made a Commander of the Order of St. John of Jerusalem. Invested by H.R.H. The Duke of Gloucester at Buckingham Palace.

1972   Invested as Dame of Grace of the Order of St. John in London by The Lord Prior, Lord Cacia.

1981   Received "Achiever of the Year" from the National Home Furnishing Association in Colorado Springs, U.S.A., for her designs for wallpaper and fabrics.

1984   Received Bishop Wright Air Industry Award at Kennedy Airport, for inventing the aeroplane-towed Glider.

1988   Received from Monsieur Chirac, The Prime Minister, The Gold Medal of the City of Paris, at the Hotel de la Ville, Paris, for selling 25 million books and giving a lot of employment.

1991   Invested as Dame of the Order of The British Empire, by H.M. The Queen at Buckingham Palace for her contribution to Literature.